SOME
PERSONAL
PAPERS

JoALLEN BRADHAM

BLACK BELT PRESS
Montgomery

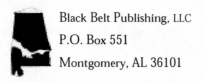
Black Belt Publishing, LLC
P.O. Box 551
Montgomery, AL 36101

A limited edition of this title was published by Texas Review
Press as the winner of the 1994 Breakthrough Award in
Southern and Southwestern Fiction; that edition won the
1996 Townsend Award.

ISBN 1-881320-95-2

Design by Randall Williams
Printed in the United States of America

*The Black Belt, defined by its dark, rich soil, stretches across
central Alabama. It was the heart of the cotton belt. It was and is
a place of great beauty, of extreme wealth and grinding poverty,
of pain and joy. Here we take our stand, listening to the past,
looking to the future.*

Some Personal Papers

For

T. A. B.

DAY ONE

I have six days to talk about seven souls. And I don't usually talk about love and pity. My training was clinical, and we had it drilled into us to be thinking, not feeling. In school they said over and over that if you cared too much, if your heart was all caught up in the mess you had to deal with, you wouldn't make it a year. I learned all that, but now I have to talk about love. The love part started it all— and finished it.

In March of 1979, I went into Building D and up the stairs to D-38. The door was standing half open, but I knocked, anyway, first softly so's not to rouse all the children on the floor, then more loudly. No sound anywhere. In a building always screaming with babies crying and drunks yelling, the silence was scary. By then, I'd been in a lot of tenements in a lot of places. I knew about silence, and I knew about noise.

My mother used to say, "Look around." My father, "Listen for God. He speaks all the time." Both spoke the truth that day.

Everything in the two-room apartment was filthy.

Food had run over the stove so the layers of crusts that coated it looked like river mud on the sides and the floor around. Piles of trash all about. An old television stood in one corner. Near it was a mattress on the floor. Blood, urine stains, and cigarette burns marked it with different circles. Like a design for some ritual; you know the kind. You see 'em on walls sometimes, under overpasses. The only other thing was the old crib where Herez was tied.

He was eleven years old but so stunted he was about the size of a five-year-old. He couldn't stretch out in the crib, but he could fit. Someone had used strips of an old sheet to tie him to the bars on both sides. He was just lying there, staring into space, the mattress badly soiled. His lips were cracked like he hadn't had any water for a time, but his hands and arms, so badly burned with cigarettes and irons the other times I'd seen him, didn't show any new scars.

I bent over and looked directly at Herez. He seemed to pull his eyes in from a long, long way to focus on my face. Then from somewhere, he made the association.

"Miss Genie," he said, trying to raise his little arms.

The silence hung everywhere. Only a rat scratching in the wall made a little scribble-scrabble.

Without any plan, I untied the rags that bound him. I took off my jacket and, lifting him, slipped it around him. It was not cold outside even though it was only early March, but the boy was frail as well as naked. I picked him up.

"Herez, darlin', how'd you like to go home with me for a few hours? Have a nice bath and some good warm soup? I bet you'd like some cheese. I remember how much you like cheese."

"Miss Genie," he said again, holding around my neck like a small animal that feared being pulled away and stuffed back in a cage.

"Well, we'll go, honey. I'll bring you back after supper."

I thought about leaving a note, but Herez was crying soundlessly, the great tears just rolling down his face, while he said over and over, in a mindless way, "Miss Genie, Miss Genie."

He was light to carry. I walked back into the hall and down the stairs, aware nobody was there to leave word with for Herez's mother. On the front steps where old women usually sat and children played, only a mangy-looking dog sat scratching.

"Now, Herez, in we go. Let's see if you can sit up like the big boy you are." He tried to do what I indicated. I put the seat belt around him and, knowing I was guilty of kidnapping, went around the car.

"Car."

"Yes, darlin'. We are going in the car. We are going to clean up and have supper and then we will come back in the car. Two rides today. Won't that be fun?"

He looked at me; nothing seemed to register or change in his face.

On my street children played, but not many adults were home from work. I knew I could use the automatic opener, pull into my garage, and close the door behind me. No one would see me.

"Herez," I said, remembering suddenly the box my sister Mary Anna had left with me. "Herez, honey, you 'sposed to visit me today. My sister left some clothes her grandson has outgrown. They'll 'bout fit you." My older sister Mary Anna, who'd come through a few weeks earlier, had left a box my younger sister Louise Lucille was supposed to pick up at Easter. "I know there's a flannel shirt. What do you say to a flannel shirt, lovey?"

"Shirt, shirt," he said in parrot fashion.

I carried him in the house and immediately wrapped him in a blanket. "We'll just make a little Indian papoose out of you."

He gurgled.

"First thing you need, sweet baby, is a glass of milk. You like a cup of warm chocolate milk?"

"Straw."

"Yes, sir, with a straw." I slipped him into the bench at the table and began heating the milk. I had no sense of his skill in language. His mental age when the clinic tested him a year earlier was about five. The psychologist had classified him as severely retarded and only marginally trainable and then under the best conditions. The recommendation was to put him in the state institution where at least he couldn't be abused and neglected, but his mother claimed she loved him and wanted him at home. We—my office, the State—could not say he was violent or dangerous.

At the moment Herez seemed alert. He had spotted the salt and pepper shakers in the shape of pigs and was trying to work his way out of the blanket to reach them.

"Here we are, Herezzie-roo; here's some milk." I put the cup down.

His face clouded. "Straw," he screamed. "Straw."

I had kept some straws from stops at the Burger Bin and went to the utensils drawer. Three straws. I cut one in two.

"Here's a straw, darlin'. Let's drink the milk. I'll pull the pigs over here to watch you. I bet those piggies would like some milk."

I put my arm around him and held the cup while he sucked slowly at the straw.

"You think you can hold the cup?" For some reason I felt obligated to help him develop motor skills. He nodded without moving his mouth from the straw. I folded back the blanket and put his hands around the cup which rested securely on the Formica surface.

"Good, Herez." I said with enthusiasm. "You're a big boy, sweetie. You hold the cup good."

"Cup."

"And the piggies will dance for you," I said, reaching for the salt and pepper shakers. "This little piggy went to market. This little piggy stayed home." I made the salt shaker dance off to market, located near the napkin holder, and drew the pepper shaker back under my cupped hand like it was staying home. Herez watched fascinated, his hand clamped around the cup, and his mouth very slowly sucking the last of the chocolatey dregs. There were little slurping sounds. Then he smiled.

"Herez, let's learn the piggy song. Say after me: 'This little piggy went to market.'"

I started again, "This . . ." He joined me hesitantly, but we said the line while I made the salt shaker dance and prance as if going to market was all that a pig heart or Herez or I could ever desire on the face of the earth.

"This little piggy went to market," he said by himself. The salt shaker ran in a circle of delight.

"Now, Herezzie-rezzie, the second line is 'And this little piggy stayed home.' Say that with me." He did and then over and over by himself while the pepper shaker ran scuttling back and back and back each time to the protective home of my left hand.

Herez laughed and gurgled in delight. The pigs were frantic.

"Say both lines, honey. Say the line 'bout going to market and the one 'bout staying home. Don't stop between the lines." I got the pigs ready for a big performance.

Herez, my boy child, almost shouted, "This little piggy went to market, and this little piggy stayed home." The pigs acted it out over and over. When I was sure he had the lines, I said, "Herez, you make the pigs dance while I wash the cup." I put his right hand over the salt shaker and his left over the pepper. He could not make them work at the same time, but finally he could say the lines and move the salt shaker to his far right and then stop and with both hands and full concentration get the pepper shaker into the top of the bread cover which I was holding up to represent home. He sagged a little.

"Herez, darlin', I think it's time for a bath and a nap. The piggies are very tired."

I picked him up and put him in the tub. As the warm water ran in around him, he patted it happily. Dirt was crusted on him and his hair was matted. I washed him carefully and scrubbed his hair. I did not see any new signs he'd been abused, but the scars from old burns were all over his little buttocks and thighs. I kept talking to him so he could learn some words. I don't know why I thought I should enrich his vocabulary; it just seemed the thing to do. We worked on *soap, towel, water, faucet*—things like that. I wanted to help him; Lord, how I wanted to help him. He was so sleepy he could not even repeat most of the words. I knew he would go straight to sleep.

I put him between the sheets of my bed and turned on the electric blanket. I watched him a few minutes. He was a café-au-lait child, dozens of shades lighter than me. The color against my forest green sheets was very soothing. Green and brown like a garden. It looked healthy and natural. I chuckled to think how funny I must look against the dark green sheets. Maybe I needed light sheets to keep from getting lost in the dark. I felt happy and very young, like a new mother who had just brought her much-wanted baby home from the hospital.

Well, I had to clothe that baby. I found the box Mary Anna had left. In addition to the worn flannel shirt were several tee-shirts with designs on them, some underwear, and a pair of corduroy pants, washed so many times they were thin like cotton. Except for shoes, I could fix my boy up well enough to take him home. Mary Anna had included some old stuffed animals which she thought Louise's boy might enjoy. A one-eared bear and a black and white dog were rolled in the Batman tee-shirt.

I softly put the bear and the dog next to Herez so he'd find them when he woke up. Then I started supper. I felt he should have soft food, although I knew at home he had to eat whatever was tossed him like a dog that didn't get fed regular and took whatever came whenever. I remembered how much he liked hotdogs at the clinic, but I didn't have any hotdogs. Tomorrow I would get some. Oh, I knew they weren't the best thing for children, but what was the harm in this boy having one thing that pleasured him? Tomorrow, for one day, he could have something he liked. No. That was silly. I had to take him back as soon as he'd finished his nap and eaten.

I found a can of cream of chicken soup and a can of applesauce. I thought I would cut the crust from a slice of bread and melt a little cheese on it. The warm soup and cheese bread and the cool applesauce would taste good and be good for him. I lined things up on the counter to be ready when he woke up.

Then I remembered that I'd kept some children's books. A few very old ones we had at home, a few I picked up to read to my nieces and nephews when they stayed with me. Somewhere in the book box was *Charlotte's Web*. Now that Herez was interested in pigs, he might be able to follow Wilbur. I was mighty happy, just at the thought of reading the book to him.

The book box was a wooden case my brother Bob had built in shop class years ago. He had put rope handles on the ends. All of us had used it for one thing or another over the years, and now it had become my book box though I intended to give it to a niece or nephew. I hauled out the box and opened it. There were enough books to read to Herez for a long time. Again I stopped and corrected myself. Here was *Charlotte's Web* to read to him just before I took him home in an hour or so. I wouldn't have time to finish it, I knew, but it seemed a good thing to start.

I went in to check on Herez. He had turned over and was sleeping with one arm over the bear. I looked at the clock. Five fifteen. I could let him sleep until six, then feed him, read the story, and take him home. His mother would be delighted that he was clean and fed. If she was home. And sober. The chances of either were small, I realized.

Molly Alexander, Herez's mother, received a little welfare check, but she made her money by a series of jobs that never lasted long and that she seldom reported. She made a little by hustling, but apparently not much. A more or less full-time guy lived with her—Horton or Homer or something like that—and he was the one who'd burned Herez before. Molly had a theatrical temper and liked to kiss and hug Herez in public and declare how much she loved her baby and that she would do anything for him. She had refused all suggestions of foster homes and the state institution, moaning, "Lord, no. A baby belong with his mama. A baby belong with his mama. This here's my baby, and I'm gonna take care of him."

Her baby was sleeping with my nephew's castoff teddy bear in my bed at this moment. I went in to check on him. He was awake and had both the dog and the bear on his chest. He was looking at them with wonder.

"Well, Herez, precious, you have some friends, I see."

"Miss Genie?" His voice stayed up, but he lacked the words for what he wanted to say.

"Yes, honey, the dog and the bear are yours. Now, let's go to the bathroom and then get dressed. Then we will name your dog and bear. Can you use the bathroom by yourself?" I asked, helping him up. He did not say anything. I helped him and tried to explain what he should do and why he should flush the toilet. He liked the flushing and wanted to do it over and over. But finally I got him into the clothes, which were a little big on his thin frame, but they served well enough and were better than the things he usually wore, or at least better than the things I had seen him in during his trips to the clinic or my visits to the housing project.

"Herez, bring Dawg and Bear and we'll have dinner."

This time I let him walk. He managed, but there was little coordination and he was very frail. In the kitchen he slipped back in the spot where he had his milk and fondled the stuffed animals while I heated the soup and fixed cheese toast. I sat down next to him. "Look, Herez, here is some cheese toast and some soup and some applesauce." I realized I'd have to feed him the soup. His coordination was so poor he couldn't manage by himself. He ate every bite.

"Say the piggy song for me. Let's see how well you remember it." With just a little coaching, he said it pretty well, and then he went over it several times.

"Hooray, Herez. Can you say that? Hooray, Herez. See, they sound alike." He made little happy noises.

"Herez, can you say your name and address?"

He looked at me without comprehension.

"My name is Herez Alexander. Say that with me. My name is Herez Alexander."

After a few tries he seemed to have it, but my sense was he was mimicking.

"I live at D-38 Calvin Court, Manchester." I knew Molly didn't have a telephone. "Darlin' baby, you want to learn this address so if you get lost you can say where you live. That way, people will find your mama or take you home."

Much good that will do, I thought. The best thing that could happen to you would be never to go back to that hole again. "Come on, say it with me: I live at D-38 Calvin Court, Manchester."

We worked on this for some time, but the ideas were harder than the piggies dancing on the table, so I took the bear and held it on the table in front of him. Then I said, "Mr. Bear, what is your name?" Herez waited a minute and said slowly, "My name's Herez Alexander." I made the bear clap its paws. "Good for you, Mr. Bear, I mean Mr. Alexander. And where do you live?" Herez tried immediately but couldn't get the number right. I didn't know how to teach him about 38 since he couldn't count. Rote memory seemed the only thing.

"Mr. Bear says, 'Thirty-eight, thirty-eight, thirty-eight.'"

I put the much-rubbed dog on the table. "And Dawg says, 'Thirty-eight, thirty-eight, thirty-eight.'" I tried to say the number as if a dog were barking.

Herez smiled with delight, his eyes wide with pleasure.

I moved the pigs into position. "And you, piggies,
what do you say?"

"Thirty-eight, thirty-eight, thirty-eight," they snorted
in unison.

"Herez, Mr. Bear, and Dawg, and the two piggies say
thirty-eight. They want you to say it with them. Come on
now. Let's go."

"Thirty-eight, thirty-eight, thirty-eight," he said.

"Wonderful. Hooray, Herez. Hooray, Herez." I leaned
over and kissed his forehead. "Now let's say the sentence.
'I live at D-38 Calvin Court, Manchester.'"

He said it, imitating me exactly. Then without any
prompting, he said the whole thing: "My name is Herez
Alexander. I live at D-38 Calvin Court, Manchester."

"Good, Herez! That's very good. You remember your
address and talk to people only if you know them." I knew
this meant nothing to him. He would go with others as
easily as he had come with me. "Don't go with people you
don't know." I did not want to frighten him, but there was
so much he needed to learn. But I knew while I tried to
teach that he had absolutely no future. His mind and his
body were permanently stunted. He was regularly abused.
The simplest education was beyond him. But I wanted to
do something for him. I wanted to give him something
better than he had ever had. If I could, I wanted to make
his future just a little more bearable than it inevitably
would be.

"Herez, I want us to read a story. Bring Mr. Bear and

Dawg in the living room, and we'll read about a pig named Wilbur. Wilbur looks like the pigs on the table 'cept he's a different color." He snuggled up beside me. Leaning against my arm and holding the stuffed animals, my new little son went to sleep. And without making a conscious decision, I set upon taking him back tomorrow. After all, it was Friday night, and his mother would be too drunk to care if I took him back now. I slipped away from him and eased him down on the couch. Then I found some blankets and covered him up. I pulled another chair with a high back against the couch so that he could not roll over and fall off.

On Saturday morning I slipped away very early and bought a few groceries and some cheap sneakers that looked about the right size. When I came back he was still asleep. I decided I'd cut his hair when he woke up. We made a production out of the haircut, and then he worked on learning how to put on shoes and tie them. He could match the shape of his foot with the shape of the shoe, but he could not tie his shoes.

I did not want to take him in the yard because of several big holes I had dug to put in azalea bushes. My brother-in-law Gus was changing the landscaping at City Center and had promised me some of the bushes they were discarding, but he said I had to have the holes ready so when his truck came, his men could drop the plants in the holes and I wouldn't have to struggle with them. If Herez wasn't here, I'd be digging now, I thought. With the holes and Herez's poor coordination, taking him out didn't seem very safe. He could easily fall in and hurt himself.

Anyway, teaching Herez some basic skills was more important than holes for azalea bushes. We could do some bending and stretching exercises in the house. We played a few minutes, but he tired very easily. Then we went back to *Charlotte's Web.* I wanted to teach him. I felt like Annie Sullivan with a different kind of deafness and blindness before me. I wanted to take his hand and make the sign for *water* or *doll.* When I got to a line that seemed easy to say, I stopped and asked Herez to say it with me. I wondered if I could make up rhymes to teach him things he could use so living would be easier. When we finished the book, I would teach him the days of week and, if possible, how to tell time. Both of these he would need. Need them. Why would he need them? He would never go to work, or punch a clock, or have a calendar. His disposition was sweet; he seemed eager to please. But we had been over and over putting him in a special school and home. His mother would not listen.

He was sitting on the floor with the bear and the dog, making some sort of sounds to them. The noises sounded happy, and on occasion he would sing to them about the piggies. Each time he sang the piggy song, I'd say, "What is your name?" and he'd reply: "My name's Herez Alexander. I live at D-38 Calvin Court, Manchester."

"Herez, we're going to have hotdogs for lunch. And an apple and a glass of milk. Sound good to you?"

"Straw?" he asked.

"Yes, my man, a straw."

I put the simple lunch together. He seemed so happy on the floor I decided to create a makeshift picnic. I spread a sheet over the carpet and told him to move himself, Mr. Bear, and Dawg to the center of it. He did. No one had ever paid so much attention to him before.

I took the little lunch to him and spread things out just like a grassy field. He saw the hotdog but didn't respond to it. The reaction struck me funny 'cause six months ago at the clinic he had loved hotdogs so much we called him the Hotdog Kid. He looked at it like he'd never seen one before. I moved it toward him, "Here, Herez, baby, here's your favorite, a hotdog. I bet Mr. Bear and Dawg would like to have one too."

He moved back just a little and looked like he was gonna cry. Not wanting to frighten him—I thought he had forgotten about hotdogs and this one scared him—I put it back on the plate. "See, Herez," I said, scraping the spoonful of chili from the top. "This is the chili. It's the topping to make the hotdog taste real good. We'll put it back after we see the parts of the hotdog. I like to know how things are put together, and I bet you like to know too." I opened the bun and with the fork pulled the weenie out. Then I picked up the bun. "See, this is the bun. The bakery makes it long like this so that it will be just the right size for the meat. Remember the way the shoes are just a little longer than your feet so they'll go around them. Well, the bun's like that."

I put the bread down and picked up the weenie with my fingers. He looked frightened. I moved it slightly toward him. "This is the weenie or frankfurter." His eyes widened in fear. He rolled into a fetal position on the floor and began to moan and whimper as if someone were hurting him. "No, Hoover. No, Hoover. No." He screamed and then sobbed.

Hoover. That was the man Molly lived with. The one who had burned Herez first with the cigarettes, then with the iron. Now, sexual abuse. Quickly I swept up the remains of the picnic and carried them to the kitchen. I came right back and sat by him.

"Herez, Herez, honey," I crooned. "Mr. Bear and Dawg don't know why you're crying. They want you to hug 'em. They miss you. You don't want to make Mr. Bear cry; I know you don't want to make Dawg sad." I said it over and over in a kind of singsong voice. After a long time, he stopped crying and whimpering and sat up next to me, leaning against me in exhaustion.

"Here," I said, "here, talk to Mr. Bear and Dawg. Tell them everything's all right." He repeated the words after me. While he made sounds, I decided that I'd keep him over the weekend and on Monday take all possible legal action to have Herez placed in a foster home. Whatever influence I had in social service agencies I would use.

Late Sunday afternoon Herez was taking a nap. I cleaned up the house and tried to plan something that would benefit Herez. I reviewed the facts about his mother. Everything was detrimental or dangerous to Herez. I recalled Hoover's record and knew the man to be sadistic and abusive. I assessed Herez's mental and physical capacities, the concepts he might come to understand, the tasks he might master. Neither his mind nor his body could provide him any kind of living. He had neither judgment nor the capacity to develop it. I held myself in check. I didn't proceed emotionally or passionately. I moved through a formal, evaluative checklist of survey, evaluation, prediction, the kind I had spent twenty years filling out and the kind that passed over my desk every day.

I went over, for what seemed the millionth time, the chances of Molly letting Herez go into an institution that could protect him. Again nothing. Court action was possible, but I knew from precedent that if the State took Herez away from his mother, even with the strong evidence in this case, return to her after a short period would be inevitable. Herez seemed bound to her and caged by her neglect.

What did Herez need? The answer came quickly because it was obvious: Herez Alexander needed freedom from the system. He needed freedom from his mental and physical deformity. Herez needed to be freed from his cage.

I thought I heard him stirring and went to check on him. The noise was the bear falling to the floor. Herez was deep in sleep.

I sat down and watched him. Asleep he looked a great deal like my little brother Alfred Andrew who had been born deformed and who died at eleven. "The Lord took him. The Lord freed him from his troubles." I could hear my father saying it over and over. "Freed him; freed him from his prison."

Daddy, though crying, preached the burying, and the old timers murmured, "Freed him, freed him," each time Daddy paused.

I shivered. A rabbit ran over my grave. That was

exactly what Herez needed. But his little heart beat steadily in his sleep. I could kill him. No. Of course I couldn't kill him. I loved him. Women like me did not kill. I had a professional and personal obligation to him. By both, that obligation was to improve his lot, to free him from the prison of D-38 Calvin Court and the bars of his body and mind. Alfred Andrew, who had known neither deprivation nor abuse, was freed.

I could see my father, old, the way he was just before his own death. He was saying in his slow deliberate speech with all the intonations and pronunciations of his time and space, "Genie, Genie, freein' is the Lord's work. You know that. Look to the Lord. Any killin' is wrong. Oh, Genie, Genie."

But those were old words and here in my charge was the abused boy.

Could I do it? Physically, yes. Herez was frail and trusting. But bringing myself to it? Choose to? Commit to? Take the step? I knew I already had. It was the only way to make a positive difference for Herez.

How? He liked to bathe so much, drowning would be easy. But I could not deal with the pain of his little lungs filling up and his terrible confusion as it happened. Already he had suffered more than most people do in a lifetime. I had no pills he could take. Perhaps there were a couple of aspirin in the house, a Tylenol or two, but all of them together would not affect even his small body. To free, not to burden, was the point. He was such a tiny, flickering light in such a terribly murky world.

I put on my blue jeans and work shirt and went in the

yard. Two of the deep holes I had made were very close together. If I made another hole between them, the overall length would be about four feet. I started digging. I felt a great surge of energy. I dug well, the dirt releasing its hold on the earth and flying in a lighthearted manner to the pile next to the hole.

"Evenin', Genia, still workin' on your yard. Shames the rest of us."

I stopped. It was Lon Bates, my neighbor. "Evenin', Lon, how you?"

"Fine, fine, just wish my yard look like yours."

"My brother-in-law Gus called to say that tomorrow he's bringing the azaleas. I'm gonna have these holes ready. He says they're real big bushes. White blooms."

"We'll like lookin' at 'em." Lon went back to changing the oil in his truck.

I kept digging, knowing I had to join the three holes, make the depth greater than any azalea bush could ever need and then create a false bottom on top where Gus would put the azalea roots. I dug with rhythm and energy, feeling a great sense of purpose and fulfillment. Everything I had ever wanted to accomplish in terms of helping children and easing their burdens was taking shape. The little light of Herez Alexander was sleeping peacefully inside. I would pull the sheet over Herez's face and then smother him with the pillow. There would be only the moment of struggle with his frail body and weak lungs; then he would be free. I finished the hole and called to Lon, "Hope when you get home tomorrow, you see a couple of good-sized bushes here."

"I'm watchin'. Next thing you be puttin' in a pool."

I laughed. "Lon, it's the Lord's truth you never seen me in a bathing suit." Then we both laughed.

I went in and started taking the books out of the book box. I was fixing to use it as a little coffin, but the box would take up far more room than the body, and if Gus dropped the bushes there was a chance the top of the box would thud. No, I'd just wrap Herez in a sheet and speed the freeing of his limbs. The little body had already known too many boxes. I put the books back in the box.

I washed my hands and face, tidied my hair. I looked at the clock. It would be dark soon. Lon and his family spent Sunday evenings glued to a television and went to bed early. As soon as it was dark I could take Herez out.

I walked over to the bed, knowing what I was to do and knowing a feeling of peace and exhilaration. My life and training and desire to help would not be wasted. I pulled the forest green sheet over his face. He didn't stir. I picked up the pillow, an old-style feather pillow I'd recovered many times. Now it looked stylish and new in the green pillow case.

"I love you, Herez. You'll never be mistreated again. Your handicaps have hurt you for the last time," I said as I put the pillow over his face and held it down. He struggled even less briefly than I thought he might. Foolishly, what kept running through my head was "This little piggy has roast beef."

He was in the little briefs and a tee-shirt that said "I Love Manchester," but the *love* was a badly faded red heart. I wrapped him in the sheet that had covered him and then stripped the rest of the bed. His little body looked like a pile of laundry waiting to be put in the washer.

I gathered the other sheet, the pillowcases, and the clothes he had worn and put them in the machine, measured the detergent, and set the dial for permanent press. Almost as soon as the churning started, the telephone rang.

"Genie, Gus. I'll be there with the bushes tomorrow. 'Less it's pourin' rain. Still want 'em where you show me?"

"Yes, Gus. Please. 'Bout what time?"

"Real early. We got to get these up and off so's we can set some trees. Real early 'fo the folks goes to work."

"So you'll come 'fo I leave, 'fo 8:00?"

"Close to 6:00, I guess. Look, gotta go. Supper's gettin' cold."

"Bye then. Thanks, Gus."

We hung up. I went for my purse to find my appointments for Monday. Nothing in the morning, but at 2:00 I was to receive an award for helping in a rezoning issue. I'd have to dress tomorrow, definitely a blue-suit day.

I transferred the clothes from the washer to the dryer and then went outside. It was almost dark enough. I remembered some lime in the garage and decided to get it. I sprinkled some in the bottom of the hole and left the bag nearby. Because of my fence I did not have to worry about dogs. I was relieved that I thought of these things in so clear and orderly a fashion. It was like I was conducting a staff meeting and had to think of all objections or alternatives before the meeting actually began. I walked up to make sure the gate was securely latched. Most people seemed to be inside and quiet. I could see TV sets blinking behind windows. I wondered how much activity there was at Calvin Court right now and what Molly was doing. Would she file a missing person report? All my instincts told me she would go along relieved unless she found an occasion to dramatize or make money on her loss.

I went in the house and without turning on any lights picked up Herez. I walked back to the edge of the hole and knelt slowly so I could place the green cocoon squarely on the ground. I wanted a simple dignity for him. I swung my legs into the hole and sat there a moment aware of the chill, the smell of earth, and the night noises, aware that my skin was part of the darkness and that, unless the whites of my eyes showed, I was a moving spirit of darkness.

All the graveside services my father had conducted came to me as I lifted Herez in the dark green sheet, and then I extended him outward and upward in tribute. I laid him in the hole and sprinkled a handful of soil over him. I whispered, "The Lord be with thee and with thy spirit." It was all I could think of. I pulled myself out and shoveled in a thin layer of dirt. I sprinkled a layer of lime and then a good bit of dirt. I walked around and packed it down hard. My weight was a great advantage to me. Then I put in more dirt loosely so the packed layer wouldn't show. I was a force of universal blackness working without effort in the caressing night.

I went back in the house, stripped off my clothes at the door, and moved through the dark hall to the bath. I bathed, washed my hair, put cream on my face, and washed the tub. In clean gown and robe, I went back to the kitchen, picked up my work clothes and shook the dirt outdoors. I put the dirty clothes in the hamper next to the washer. Then I took the dry things out of the dryer. I folded the clothes from Mary Anna's box. Then I unfolded the shirt the stuffed animals had been rolled in, went for the animals, and arranged them as I had found them. I replaced the box. I folded the green sheet and the matching pillowcases, put them in the linen closet and pulled out a white set to make my bed.

Next morning before I put on my blue suit, I swept the back porch. When Gus came I was ready for work except I had on my yard shoes.

"Good Lord, Genie, I got big men that can't dig a hole like this."

"Been doin' it along, but yesterday I really worked at it. You say be ready and I'm ready."

"Honey, you always ready. That's why yo' folks so proud of you."

His men swung two good-sized bushes into the long hole and kicked some dirt in. Then they put the other plants in the other holes in the yard.

"That's OK, Gus, I'll fill in the holes when I get home this afternoon. I'm dressed for work now."

"Why you so dressed up? Look like you fixin' to preach. Alma Faye says all the time you ought to take to preachin'. You can get that rise-and-fall voice the preachers use, and you know all the old Bible words and phrases. Says you sound like yo' daddy, just preachin' away and usin' all the right words and sounds." Realizing his men could hear him, he stopped. He tried to keep his soft side hidden from the men.

"I'm just going to a little ceremony. That's all. Got to have more than a jar full of memorized phrases to be a real preacher."

"Yo' folks sho' be proud of you, all the same. Alma Faye says that all the time." He looked toward his men, who were getting in the back of the truck. "Well, we gotta go."

"Thanks, Gus. Maybe y'all can come for dinner next Sunday."

"Have to ask Alma Faye 'bout that. 'Spec so, though. I know if you jes stick yo' finger in the stew, it taste mighty good. Bye."

At home that evening, I filled the dirt around the azaleas, offered each shovelful as a tribute to Herez. While I ate a little supper, I let the water feed slowly into the earth, through the dark green hose blessing and cleaning.

"Herez, Herez, you part of freedom. I love you," I whispered into my kitchen.

Life went on after Herez came to live with me. My new azaleas did well in the spring and summer. I spent a few days in May visiting my folks near North Augusta, about five miles from where I grew up, and meeting my new great-niece, named Eugenia for me. In August I went to Chicago for the funeral of my oldest sister Elizabeth and stayed the weekend with Alexandra, a niece I never knew I had until I became Director of the Office of Children's Services in Manchester, and she wrote me from her social

services office. She saw the announcement in a professional journal. A nice surprise greeted me as soon as I came
back to the office. My staff bought the supplies and paid
for the framing, and one of the women who was good at
needlepoint made a lovely piece for me. They hung it next
to my door while I was away. When I turned from seeing
it the first time to ask my secretary about it, ten or twelve
people were watching me and grinning. The needlepoint
said: "Don't tell me about cases; tell me about children."
It meant more than all the awards I'd ever received, more
than the letter of commendation from the Governor for
my reorganization of the programs in Children's Services,
even more than the testimonial dinner at the Yonak Street
YMCA in November.

At Christmas, I drove over to North Augusta to spend
Christmas with my sister Mary Anna and her extended
family. On the morning after Christmas I wanted to see
the new house my niece Martha was in, but I didn't know
the way. New roads seemed to shoot off in all directions so
the country hardly looked at all like what I knew. Martha
said she'd meet me at the Kmart and lead me the rest of the
way.

I sat waiting on the benches in the front of the store.
The place reinforced all my feelings that the day after
Christmas was the saddest day of the year, when everybody faces the truth that no gift brings the dream and no
string of light makes any difference in the dark. The
desperate faces come back the day after Christmas. It hurts
mighty hard when you want something but it don't come.
I saw that hurt all 'round me that morning. In the Kmart

after Christmas you see lots of folks know the dream's not coming.

That morning, near me, a woman was talking to a man in low tones but loud enough for me to hear. In a funny, hard accent, he cursed and said she had to go with him. A baby, covered by a faded and dirty Peter Rabbit blanket, slept in a plastic carrier next to her. Only a little of its face was exposed. The woman seemed aware of the need to protect the little life from the elements. A cap covered the baby's forehead and ears. The Peter Rabbit blanket was pulled up over the cheeks. Only the tiny mouth, the little button nose, and the sleeping eyes were visible. All the customers coming and going in the area did not faze the infant, who slept silent and unstirring.

The woman stood up to go over to the water fountain. She was one of those pigeon-shaped women with a large protruding bosom kinda cantilevered with a oversized rear. The tight stretch pants with an elastic waist and the big print knit blouse showed off everything. Since I was on the side of the handle of the drinking fountain, I could see her hand turn the wheel. Three fingers had long gold nails and each finger, several rings. She pretended to drink water much longer than she actually did, like she needed to stall and had nowhere to go. Eventually, she turned back to her seat, and I saw the other hand had all bright-red nails, not so long and pointy as the gold ones. Each finger seemed to have at least two rings.

"We come this far. Do what I say or get the hell out."

"But . . . ."

"Don't but me. Do what I say and we cut. Come noon

we be in Florida; we start clean. Can't afford nothin' that slow us down. Nothin'."

She kept looking at the baby.

"Who's to know?" he said. He started getting up.

"Aunt Genie, Aunt Genie," Martha burst in. "Aunt Genie, I'm sorry I made you wait, but we had to boost the battery. Come on. I'm in front. The baby's in the car. Where you parked?"

I wanted to stay so I could at least get the tag number on the couple's car, but Martha's anxiousness swept me out of the building and back into the parking lot.

I spent the day with Martha admiring the house and playing with her new daughter, little Genie, but all the time thinking about the couple and the baby in the Kmart.

"Martha," I said, "I need to leave 'bout 3:00. I'd like to get back 'fo it's so late and dark. Lots of people goin' back tonight, you know. Traffic'll be bad."

"Aunt Genie, I wish you'd stay over. Little Genie needs your influence. You could leave tomorrow."

I hugged the baby, whose eyes followed my earrings with wonder. "This baby needs hugs and snuggles and the sound of your voice. That's what this precious baby needs. And I need to go. For me this has been a long trip—three days away."

She laughed. "I declare, Aunt Genie, you're too conscientious. Nobody takes work so serious the way you do. Mother says you were always like that." Then she took on the voice they all use to mimic me, "Doin' right hold steady." We both laughed.

"Well, I guess I'm just too old to change now."

"I'll lead you to the expressway if you really got to go."

Then I said without planning to, "If you'll tell me how to get back to the Kmart, I can find my way from there. Didn't seem far to the Kmart, just winding in these new streets."

"No. It's some shorter than our exit. But I still wish you wouldn't go. I love you, Aunt Genie; you know we all do." She embraced me and kissed me like I was her mother, not her aunt. "You've done a lot for us. You know, given us a chance to move up."

But I left. I drove to the Kmart. Before I got out of the car, I put on my ski cap and pulled it low down around my ears; I turned up my coat collar. The weather had turned real cold, and no one around there knew me. I didn't have to worry 'bout setting a good example or being a role model.

I went in the store which was still crowded, by now with those who'd been working all day. The atmosphere was even sadder than it had been that morning. Those who had put in a day's work knew that nothing had been changed by the Christmas day they dreamed of. All they knew was that their debts were greater and their dream was dead.

I took a buggy and began going up and down the aisles very slowly, you know what I mean, like a lady with a long shopping list and all the time in the world. I knew the baby would be there. I also knew that clerks and security people had seen it and chosen to ignore it 'cause ignoring it was the easy out—no judgment, no giving names and dates and places, no extending the self, no blurring of what you had to do between what folks call the hell-moment of clocking in and the joy-moment of clocking out. But I was already bound to that infant that slept somewhere in the Kmart, in the plastic carrier with the Peter Rabbit blanket.

There the carrier was, propped in a shopping buggy at the end of the aisle by the auto parts, just the place not many women interested in babies would stop. The infant, still with eyes closed and wearing its cap, breathed very softly and rhythmically. It needed changing. I hated the couple for abandoning the helpless bit of life.

And at Christmas, too, I snorted to myself, remembering my father's Christmas sermons and his love of talking about the sweet coming of a child. Here the couple was, just passing through. They were travelers or tourists, so to speak, like Mary and Joseph. But this baby—oh my—this baby . . . . I hated these people for what they were doing to life. If they had walked up now, I think I would have killed them. Why did people cause suffering, when things were hard enough by themselves? Why did we make things worse? All my usual questions rose in fury as I swung the carrier into the shopping cart, picked up several boxes of Pampers and jars of baby food and bottles and nipples, checked out, and started for Manchester. Well up the road, I pulled into a well-lighted area to change the baby and discovered it was blind.

I passed my hand back and forth in front of its eyes. I took the flashlight from the glove compartment and bounced the light from different spots on the interior of the car. No response. I changed the diaper. And though I knew better than to reach major conclusions from a few

minutes in a highway rest area, I already knew that Peter—
I named him for his blanket, you see—had no muscle
tone; the little arms and legs were like soft rubber.

Driving on behind the beam of my headlights, I
cursed the dark, not the December night around me, but
what had been done to the innocent, the helpless, the
children who came unchoosing but cursed. I started beating my fist against the steering wheel in silent futile
protest. Peter lay mute next to me. I stopped beating the
wheel and put my right hand on his cheek. Perhaps he
could find or feel a little something of love or care or
compassion coming through my hand.

Reaching home, I put Peter in a nest of pillows so that
he would be safe and warm until the heat, which I had
turned down, came up to make the house snug. I unloaded
the car. Then I had to devote myself fully to the baby. I
glanced at the clock. Midnight—the moment between
December 26 and 27. The moment for finding out what
I could of the Christmas child.

First I examined the Peter Rabbit cover to see if it had
any kind of identification, even some laundry mark that
could help me find a city Peter's mother might come from.
Then I ripped it open. I remembered the look on the
woman's face as she struggled with her decision. I thought
she might have scribbled something and stuck it through
the loose seams. The outside covers with the faded rabbits
on them came away from the old shredded batting like
only a few threads still connected them. No slip of paper,
no identifying token lay in the rags. I took off Peter's
clothes and examined each piece carefully. Nothing that

could link him with a name, a place, a person. Only his small brown body remained. I covered him with a clean, soft wrap and went for a pan of soapy water. Then I cleaned him. I did not try to put him in the pan or take him to a basin because it was clear that he could not sit, and, even propped, he collapsed or slid downward. He seemed to have no bones, but I could feel them and see the little ribs in the thin body. I wiped him slowly with the warm water. I felt like a girl caring for a rubber doll that looked like a baby but was only a rubbery form in the shape of a baby.

I held Peter against me, cradled as if I would give him a bottle. I had bought the baby food, but now I wondered if I needed a formula. I offered a spoonful of custard, which he took, then a little more. When he had all he seemed able to deal with, I put him down and fixed him a bottle of water. He sucked it.

Well, here's Peter in my life, I thought as I took a bath. I'd need to get more food for him. And diapers. And care. Peter needed constant care. Probably professional medical care. I was reasonably sure what a medical diagnosis would be. He was born without a brain, least the way we think of a brain. All the signs were of a hydrocephalic. The brain didn't work like a brain, controlling, sending signals. It was there but not doing him any good. Then I hated his mother even more. All that fluid could have been drained if she'd had care or if she cared. Peter didn't have to be a child out of some dark past. Science could have taken care of him, but his mother had to take care of him first. I watched Peter and saw all the running and laughing he wouldn't ever do. He would never be able to talk, walk, or stand, or sit unsupported. The life expectancy a year. I'd read dozens of reports on similar infants handled by the agency; I had seen many babies in similar condition. Usually they were institutionalized for the few months they lived. In the morning I could make the right calls, get Peter in an institution, explain what had happened, and go on with my life. Being head of the Office of Children's Services had its advantages and its connections, and I would use them to see that Peter received all he could.

I changed Peter again and fixed his pillows. He had a snug place for this night, perhaps the safest of his life, and he wasn't going anywhere.

But Peter and I moved toward the New Year together, and on New Year's Eve we celebrated without horns or hats. I knew, and Peter lived, the truth that the New Year would not be substantially different from the old. Not long after midnight, Peter's head slipped sideways so that his mouth and nose were against one of the pillows in his little nest. I came into the room and realized his breathing was difficult because of his position and the pillow. Moving the pillow would have been easy; leaving it where it was was kind. Very quickly Peter was dead. I recognized and assumed full responsibility. I saw the pillow. I knew what was happening. What would happen. I chose to care by not moving the pillow. I chose to free Peter from the multiple layers of darkness in which he lay.

For the new year—freedom. He could begin again. He was the true New Year's baby, bright and starting out with no handicaps, the very baby that the old calendars used to show next to the long-bearded old year.

But because of Herez, I hesitated to bury Peter in the garden. I saw, of course, what it looked like—a nice suburban garden with the bodies of two black infants in it. It was the sort of thing those low-class papers next to the checkout line in the grocery stores gloried in, and all I wanted to do was help two frail boys no one else would. I had to honor Peter's little body that weighed no more than that of a cat.

I remembered from a long time ago a place not too far on the other side of Barnesville, you know, down towards Macon, that had always seemed off by itself and beautiful. The remains of an old house, long-ago deserted, were there, but around the house were trees that made the site special. A grove of magnolias grew in close, dark green splendor. They had been there for centuries and looked like no one had ever cut any limbs. They grew close to the ground and shaggy, the broad waxy leaves unfurling and rising as they chose, the heavy odor of the blooms filling the space with incense.

If no one had bought and developed the place since the last time I saw it, I could take Peter and hang him in a basket high in one of the magnolias. Even three feet up dogs could not reach him, and up there in the glowing green, now shiny with January frost, time and nature would take care of him.

The old produce basket seemed right for turning Peter to a nonexistence far better and easier than the brief existence he'd known. I could wrap him in one of the dark green pillowcases, put him in the basket, and hang him in the magnolias. I remembered hearing, at some point, that magnolias had been around since the time of the dinosaurs. Roots that ancient appealed to me. Peter might have a kind of home and inheritance that was majestic and deep-rooted.

Leaving the house about 5:00 A.M., I followed I-75 south and then wound from the exit to other roads into the bleak countryside. Counting on the road into the old site being there the way I remembered it, I kept going to the point the gravel road ended, and then I struck out on foot across the stiff grass and layers of leaves. It was very cold. Every night the temperature had been in the teens, and at noon a high reading of twenty-eight or thirty had been considered good. Weather not fit for this part of the country. The forecast was that the cold, hard weather would continue. Everything seemed frozen, caught in some invisible shield.

My breath made dense puffs as I crunched across the open area. I was certainly conspicuous, a large, bundled-up, middle-aged black woman carrying a produce basket. Anyone looking—any hunter who happened to be out— would hear and see me. Hearing was easy in the vast stillness that I felt went on, universe-wide and deep enough to bridge the stars to the center of the earth. But I realized with a sudden comfort that anyone seeing me would fit me into the landscape right off. I was only what I appeared to be—a large, bundled-up, middle-aged black woman carrying a produce basket that could hold any routine provision—turnips, maybe, or fat kindling wood. I was one of hundreds looking the same way and braving the cold in the same manner at this time. Nobody around here would know I was anything but what I looked.

I shifted the basket to my other hand. No vehicles were visible. There was no sign of new roads having been cut or anyone passing this way. The region was as desolate as it was cold. It simply spread out—silent, sparse, frozen. To no living thing could it offer harbor.

My heart was beating rapidly because the cold required more energy than I had thought it would. I knew I had about two miles to go. My heavy shoes were lined with fur and very comfortable. I looked behind me. My foot prints trailed me with the stride of someone with a mission. The earth was stone hard, of course, but the frost-set print on the packed and decomposing leaves recorded my quest for the magnolias.

Then I could see them, the grove, as thick and dark as I remembered, rising in a circle that some lover of trees or of privacy had tended back when people first moved into this area. The trees had dropped their cones, and the volunteer magnolias had sprouted, claiming whatever light they could to grow and spread out their heavy shield-like leaves.

I moved carefully into the grove. Breaking any of the heavy branches seemed sacrilegious. This place might be the primitive grove of some African rite and ritual, and violation of a single branch might, I feared, bring down the wrath of some god of a past I did not know. On the other hand, I had no fear of something finding me. That someone else could be lurking or hiding in the protective foliage did not occur to me.

Finding a tree that seemed old and thick enough to suit me took a few minutes. Then, there it was in front of me. I moved very carefully into its trunk and looked up. I could climb four or five limbs easily and hang Peter on a broken branch above my head. The location of the broken limb seemed providential. The only possible danger was slipping on the frosty bark. But I hoisted myself slowly up as high as I needed to go and then saw an even better cradle hook for little Peter. I went up two more limbs and lifted the handle of the basket over the stob. I let myself down and very carefully stepped in my own tracks. I looked up from the ground; the basket was invisible. The green-leaved towers of the magnolias, steely in the frost, soared above me like the spires of those churches in the history books. And the love of my father, long dead now, the old country preacher, came back. There in the frost-laden desolation I said softly, "I will lift up mine eyes unto the hills." I wished I could say more and be a part of the strong trees that stood in the protective circle.

I walked back in my own tracks, carefully putting toe to heel. The strange print followed me. In looking back at the coming-and-going tracks, something of my past caught up with me of its own will. It rose and sang from my childhood, and my mother sang, too, sang again after the decades of silence.

Hush-a-bye, baby, on the tree top,
When the wind blows the cradle will rock;
When the bough breaks the cradle will fall,
Down will come baby, cradle, and all.

That was Peter, my baby, cradled in the top of the ancient magnolias. "Hush-a-bye, hush-a-bye," the wind sang softly in response. "Hush-a-bye, hush-a-bye." I heard the sound of boots on frost and leaves returning in the alto: "Hush-a-bye, hush-a-bye."

I got in the car. I might be parked on the launching pad of the moon for all the activity that occurred. Everything was eerie white, and finding a dot for the sun was impossible.

I drove to one of those places around Forsyth where the Florida-bound travelers stay, and ordered a good breakfast. I needed the hot coffee to restore some warmth to my body. Although I'd been up all night, I wasn't sleepy. On my drive back, rain began just about the time I passed the exit that earlier had taken me to Barnesville. The rain would erase my tracks in the leaves, but it would also freeze, making the road slick and dangerous and making little Peter, aloft in the tree, a hard shape wrapped in a green pillowcase. But the rain was also the cleansing agent. It was Peter's baptism into his new freedom where he would see, and where desertion couldn't happen. I drove as fast as I dared so I could get back to Manchester before everything iced over.

As soon as I came back to my house, I looked at my yard. Everything was frozen, of course, but gardeners know they must use every season, and, besides, I had to plan a shrine of some sort to Peter.

First I checked the tender plants. On the azaleas Gus had transplanted I added mulch because Herez, I felt, might need extra cover and, at any rate, his spirit would enjoy the fuss of my attention.

The peonies, being cold-loving plants, did not mind the ice. They welcomed it as I welcomed the lush balloon bloom of the flowers when their time came. What I needed was to plant something for the birds so when they came in a month or so they'd find lunch ready for them and then stay and eat the bugs for me in summer. The bright birds above Herez would be like a great mobile above the crib of a baby.

Little Genie, my namesake in North Augusta, would have many mobiles to dance above her crib and delight her eye. In fact, I would mail her one tomorrow, I decided then. One made of birds—bright cardinals and jays, yellow canaries, and chartreuse and orange parrots. They would spangle and dazzle over her, and she could learn her colors as well as the shapes and names as she reached for them.

And Peter, suspended in the ancient magnolias, had his birds that would fly over and nest with him, but he needed something in the garden, something to keep his memory green and to link him with his older brother Herez. When the frost broke for a mild spell, I should be able to smell the Christmas honeysuckle on the back fence and the wintersweet, with its bright leaves, near the door. Its leaves would also be bright in July. Those wintery smells—fresh and wonderful—would be part of the legacy of Peter. And with a final thaw in February, I'd plant three white dogwoods over on the right, in the area I was making my white garden. No. It just came to me. Each month until next December 26, I would put something white-blooming in my white garden. Each would be a shrine to Peter, who never saw light nor white nor bright. I would give him that, too. In March, white clematis to grow tall for him since he couldn't have done it on his own. Next December, the long-stalked Christmas rose would bloom for my Christmas child.

Day Two

When I was a little girl and my folks wanted me to think positively about my future—and that was no small dream back then—I fixed on two things. First thing, the really big thing, was to be a horticultural or landscape designer. Why this came to me, I don't remember now. We all worked in the garden. We had to. And out behind the house in the big field, we had corn and beans and squash. Some melons and lots of tomatoes. We ate it and sold it. I was always working in the earth, digging, planting, weeding, taking in the produce. Alma Faye liked to do canning, so we swapped off. I worked her time in the garden and field, and she did my time at the canning. The hard work in the soil was an everyday thing, but I loved the earth. Momma and Daddy wanted me to think of moving up, of finding something other than working the field or tending some white lady's house. Back then, teaching seemed about all we could reasonably expect, but loving the earth so much, I hit on horticulture. Might of been the big word I loved so much, but I knew the state college for colored had a little agriculture department. Only men, far as I knew then, took it, but that didn't worry me too much. I could outwork my brothers any day. When I saw the big gardens at the old houses, something told me I just had to find a way to become a landscape architect. Nobody I knew knew anything about it. I didn't have a prayer for horticulture or landscape design, not in the 1940s as a black girl growing up near the Georgia-South Carolina line. Momma and Daddy tried to explain things to me. I caught on.

In school we read some things by Langston Hughes and James Weldon Johnson, and I thought for a while I had to write. I know now that millions of little girls have that dream, but then, in my circle of hard work and low expectations, no one thought about being a writer. For maybe a year, it made me special.

I wouldn't have known as much as I did about either gardens or writing except Daddy was a preacher and Momma taught in the little elementary school for colored children. They read to us, and we children were encouraged to read every minute we could find.

Daddy was a Baptist preacher, but, of course, in his day no black man could make a living preaching and marrying and burying the dead. So he painted houses for ready cash. Folks used to laugh at him, saying dark as he was there was no problem he'd have a painter's red nose, at least not so anybody could see. But he never touched a drop of liquor. Thought it was wrong and taught all of us it was wrong. He took a few college courses at Orangeburg State, but he never graduated.

My momma did. With a fierce will and a course here

and a course there, with a term out for this baby or that, she finally took a degree and taught. Always in a black school, of course. She was dead before schools around there were forced to integrate.

Momma and Daddy, the teacher and the preacher, had eight children: Sam, Jr., killed in World War II; Elizabeth Mayra, who married a man named Tim Smith and went to Detroit just after the war; Chauncey Bob, who's a high school coach now; Mary Anna, who married Jack Braw and teaches high school social studies in North Augusta. Then I came along. Then Alma Faye, who runs the office for Gus's business—it's really the business of both of them. They've built up a landscape service that works all over Manchester and surrounding counties. Alma Faye answers the phone, keeps the books, does the insurance, all the desk things so Gus can be out with the men on the job. Gus wanted to be a TV comic. He rolls his eyes and says, "Lordy me. I'm just a joint venture in fertilizer and digging holes." But he works hard at his business and is real proud of his success.

After Alma Faye came Louise Lucille, who wanted to sing professionally, but settled for motherhood and a steady job with the state. The last child, Alfred Andrew, was born deformed. His mind developed very little and he died when he was eleven. So my folks, Marge and Sam Putman—the Reverend and Mrs. Samuel Adam Putman— weren't too lucky in their sons since only Bob lived to maturity, but they always said that of all their children, not one had gone bad. In their time and place, that meant a whole lot.

They wanted us to do better, to get an education, to have professions. I'll always remember the first time I heard my momma say *profession*. Her tone changed, sounded like she was saying some holy word and the Lord might strike her for getting above her raising. When my time came, some magic must of worked. Banks College, a fine old school for black women, found me and I found Banks. And there I found what Eugenia Diane Putman had to do, and it wasn't design gardens or write poetry. Then the war came, and, like a good many other colored, as we said then, I went north, charged with the new sense of freedom World War II brought us. I left for New York, but it wasn't for bright lights; I headed straight to enroll in the Masters of Social Work program at what was then New York State College in Buffalo, where I took the degree in 1950.

In 1975, having been Director of Social Services in Connecticut, I came closer home as Director of the Office of Children's Services for Manchester. The pay was less and the range not statewide, but I wanted to come back home, to help children that were *my* children. So I had a lot of meetings and a lot of conferences, all for children and services to children. And more than once, a conference wound up with a child who gave me reason to go on, to keep working hard. And true to form, a conference took me to my third boy child.

That Thursday, Friday, and Saturday I had to lead a conference on child abuse. We held it at the new branch just added to Children's Services. It was in a part of town where serious drug problems and a high crime rate made

the news every time the papers needed a story. My work—
on the site, not counting all I had done in preparation—
began when I had to open the event on Thursday evening,
introduce the speakers, all the usual stuff. As part of the
closing session on Saturday night, I had to deliver a
summary speech. After the official program closed, there
was to be a reception. Seeing all was cleared off and closed
up was my responsibility, too. The conference went well,
no hitches, except time, that is. It was after midnight when
I left the building, and the temperature was way below
freezing. I was as exhausted and cold as I ever remember
being. All I wanted to do was get home and crawl under
the electric blanket.

I'd turned from a side street into the main road that
led to the interstate, where I felt safer at that time of night,
when my headlights picked up a small figure wandering by
himself down the traffic island. He swayed back and forth,
then slumped and fell, halfway into the street. I pulled up
next to the island, got out, and helped him up. Under the
strong street light, I recognized him as Guaraldi Giles, a
little boy I'd seen several times—one of the children
already habitually on drugs. His mother, Joy Giles, was a
user and a hooker, or at least she had been at one time, I
knew.

"Guaraldi," I said, "it's Miss Genie. You remember
me. We had a visit not long ago. You remember the little
red car in my office. You sat in the car. Remember me?"
He didn't respond. "Can you tell me where you live? I'll
take you home."

He looked at me and, while silent, he didn't seem

frightened. I helped him up and into the car.

"Now, let's try hard, Guaraldi. Where do you live?"

"Nick's," he said in a dull voice.

It's an ugly night spot, with cheap, trashy apartments up over it. Real rough. I wanted to find a policeman to go with us, for safety and in case of questions, but Guaraldi was shivering and the hour was late, so I decided to risk it. We were only about four blocks away.

Nick's itself was comparatively quiet, but as soon as I reached the steps to the apartments, I knew why the boy was out wandering the streets. I asked a man on the steps which apartment was Joy Giles's. He pointed and then laughed. I knew I would recognize her when I saw her. She would remember me.

"Hey, Beaver Lady," she said, weaving over to me. She laughed, pleased at her wit. "Hey, Beaver Baby, you gettin' any?" Her several gold-tipped teeth flashed in and out, glinting in ancient voodoo charm, like she was trying to work some magic in the thick smoke of the place. The room was dim and swirling behind her, and I felt I was on the edge of some cliff, that if I took one step, little Guaraldi, who was hiding behind me and holding on around my leg, and I would fall off together into space.

The air was heavy with drugs. Its smell put me in mind of the first stages of an electric fire. My practical sense signaled me to look out for hot wires, but I knew the smell was what the people crowded into the room were using.

"Say, Beaver Baby, I bet you don't never get none. You ain't the fuckin' type. Hey," she called over her shoulder, "Hey, Buzz, get your ass over here. Here's a real big lady what wants some meat. You could get aholt here, man, I mean get aholt. Like fuckin' some mountain." The laugh shrilled up again and crackled over the hazy space.

"Ms. Giles," I said firmly. "I've brought Guaraldi home. I found 'im wandering down the traffic island." I reached around and tried to detach the boy's hand. Joy Giles looked at me as if I were speaking in a strange tongue she did not plan to learn. Her eyes were flat and wide with no comprehension, but she kept moving her mouth in a strange twitching way so her gold teeth winked in and out, sending witching signals.

"I said, I found Guaraldi outside. Wandering down the traffic island. Ms. Giles, it's past midnight. This is an eight-year-old boy. He's your son. It's below freezing outside."

She continued to stare and then, without a flicker of comprehension, turned awkwardly from me and, almost lumbering, moved back into the acrid mist and the jumble of voices and half-human sounds. I could see the outlines of people, but the odor was suffocating and the smoke stung my eyes so bad I couldn't make out much.

I twisted around to undo Guaraldi's hands from my leg. Then I took his hand and we went back down the alley. I knew I'd be killed. It was a place for muggings and bodies left lying alone in the subfreezing hours. But we got to the car. I opened the driver's side, practically stuffed Guaraldi in and threw myself after him. I locked the door and sat trembling, partly from the cold, some from fear. And mostly with indignation that this child had been so abused and neglected—by the mother who flashed her gold teeth in a drugged stupor.

I pulled myself together and started the car. I gave thanks to the Lord that night for the engine turning over and for the sudden comfort of headlights streaming out before me. In the deserted streets I drove swiftly, desperate to get out of that section, away from its sights and sounds and smells.

Guaraldi had both thumbs in his mouth; he hadn't said a word.

"Are you cold, Guaraldi?" I asked as gently as I could. I knew he was. His clothes were thin and skimpy. I turned the heater up.

"Put your feet over where the air is blowing. You can get warm that way."

He didn't move.

"Sleepy?" No answer. "Guaraldi, would you like some nice scrambled eggs before you go to bed?" No answer. He seemed catatonic.

He followed me slowly into the house. I quickly made up the couch into a bed for him. "Guaraldi, do you want something to eat?" Without answering, he dropped like a rock, too drugged to stay conscious any longer.

I brought a warm washcloth and wiped his face and cleaned his hands as well as I could. I slipped off his canvas shoes and felt his feet. Stone-cold, poor child. I wiped them and then filled the hot water bottle and tucked the covers around the bottle at his feet. He was breathing in a slow, rhythmic way, with a quality of peace and relaxation. His olive-tan skin was smooth and beautiful. I remembered a Bible verse my father used to read about someone's skin being rare and golden. I understood from looking at Guaraldi what such a description meant.

Why? I kept wondering. Why? Why do the children suffer? I wanted to heal them all, not just care for this one over the weekend and then have to turn him over to the city home. With Joy Giles's lifestyle there would be no question of protective custody. With her drug record, we could take Guaraldi from her and find a place to care for him. Guaraldi was a bright boy who could profit from care and education. He had no physical handicaps. Nothing was against him except his environment. And the drugs, destroying his mind.

I thought about Joy Giles's police record and the conferences I'd had with the caseworkers. As policy, we sent a policeman to the apartment with a caseworker because, a couple of years earlier, Joy attacked one of them with a broken bottle.

At 4:00 A.M. I left Guaraldi's side and crawled in the bed, not sleepy now but so tired my body felt I'd been beaten all over for a long time. The circle of conferences and children ran in my head, and my past kept rising and repeating. Doors had opened for me and closed, and I had opened doors for others. I still knew I had opened, not closed, doors for Herez and Peter. I dozed off but woke up at 6:00. I lay there, worrying over what doors could open for Guaraldi. He was bright and able, not like Herez and Peter, but already shadowed. Not saying anything except "Nick's" mystified me. Usually he talked and chattered away to himself when no one else was around. The house surrounded me in silence. The whole neighborhood was quiet. I got up and went in the living room. Guaraldi lay there, part of the perfect peace of Sunday morning, like a normal boy enjoying the treat of sleeping in. Then I looked more closely. He was dead.

I had before me the explanation to the police and the coroner; I had the ordeal of Joy Giles. But Guaraldi at least had solved his problem. I stood looking at the empty temple of the boy's body. How beautiful he might have been. I picked up the hot-water bottle, now cold and lifeless, from the child's feet.

Then I called the chief of police. He came himself. On my testimony and the medical evidence, there was no question of cause or guilt. The police arrested Joy Giles. At her trial, I testified to my action that Saturday night. A chronic offender, she was sentenced to five years.

As soon as the police and the medical investigator carried Guaraldi's body out of my house that Sunday morning, I went to my office. I turned on the computer and found the code number under which everything about Guaraldi and his mother was filed. In the main record, I found a long, depressing file. Children's Services had been attempting to help Joy Giles and Guaraldi for years. The record showed repeated drug abuse and regular arrests. Then I read:

Ms. Giles and her companion John Stanley were charged with forcing cocaine and other drugs on Guaraldi Giles, six-year-old son of Joy Giles. When the boy collapsed in the street, police rushed him to Central

State Hospital, where he remained in intensive care for three days.

I flipped over and glanced at the part of the hospital record the caseworker had obtained and affixed to her report. Then I skimmed the rest of the folder. I was dealing with a child and a lost life, not a folder. That's the thought that kept beating out over and over in my head.

Joy had served a short sentence for abusing the child, and Guaraldi had been put in protective custody. Unprepared for what I saw, I came upon an entry put in two days earlier, on Friday.

Guaraldi Giles, who has been in a foster home during his mother's prison term, is to spend a trial weekend with her, beginning today at 5:30. I'm to pick him up at the foster home shortly before that time. Although the physical environment has not improved, Ms. Giles hasn't used drugs for approximately 18 months and claims a strong love for Guaraldi. She understands this weekend is a trial visit and his returning to her custody depends on her behavior this weekend and on subsequent weekends. She agrees I will pick the boy up at 4:00 Sunday afternoon.

Attached was the document showing Joy Giles's scrawled name.

So, he was with her on a trial basis. She had been out of prison only a month, and this was a first weekend for Guaraldi to stay with her. That meant there was a caseworker on duty to follow up and return Guaraldi to the foster home. Liz Bufkin was the caseworker. Today she would need her considerable experience. I dialed her number.

"Liz. Genia Putman. I'm sorry to break in on your Sunday with trouble, but I have to."

"Not Guaraldi Giles?"

"Yes. How did you know?"

"When I took him to his mother Friday, he was so unhappy about staying I thought something would go wrong. I gave him money and had him memorize my number. He was to call me if he wanted to leave. He's so bright I knew he could find a phone and call."

"He's dead."

Waiting for Liz to get to the office, I looked back at the record and saw early interviews with Joy Giles had been recorded. I went to the tape file, pulled the cassette, and inserted it in the player. In the stillness of a Sunday afternoon, a near maniacal laugh rose from the whirring tape. Then the voice:

> I don't want to be here, and I don't want you or no big fuckin' agency runnin' my life. Butt yo' ass out. Butt out fo' good. Guaraldi's my boy and what I says, he does. Period.

The caseworker—this was some years before Liz—replied in a modulated professional voice but one that showed the strain of the situation.

Our purpose is to protect Guaraldi, who is a minor. He can't speak for himself or protect himself. We want to work with you, Ms. Giles, in doing what's best for Guaraldi. We are your helpers. Certainly we do not work against you.

The maniacal laugh swelled again. I heard the interviewer in what was clearly a stalling tactic which she hoped would both elicit information and calm the client, say softly, "Guaraldi's a pretty name. Tell me about it."

"It's his bastard pa." The tape whirled away in a laugh.

I clicked it off so that silence in the office settled in like a fog. Of course. I remembered hearing this scene. Andrea Hoffman, the caseworker then, had retold it with drama. No wonder Joy's flashing gold teeth seemed especially familiar. Andrea had made much of the gold teeth dancing out of the broad face when Joy Giles screamed her violent conclusion: "That goddamned Italian was his pa. Goddamned son-of-bitch Italian prick."

DAY THREE

During the summer term, I went down to Newboro State College to lead some seminars on health and human services. My letter and contract said I was the "outside consultant," a term that struck me funny, but I talked about what I knew, about a pretty long stretch in human services I'd spent about as "inside" as you can get. I didn't know what I was supposed to be outside of, but I'd filled out enough government forms not to expect too much sense. If they wanted to call me the janitor emeritus, it was all right. The doing, not the calling, made sense to me. And I was helping folks understand what I believed in. I liked all those concerned young people who looked at me with their dreams in their eyes and asked earnest questions about how to change the world. I remembered myself; I remembered all my friends when we started out in a moment drunk with postwar hope. After the final session on a Friday, the faculty members took me to an all-you-can-eat seafood buffet at a motel across from the campus. Well I must of taken the all-you-can-eat too far, or the fish was bad; anyway, I had to ask my hostess if I could lie down a spell before fixing to drive back. We went to the campus, and I stretched out in the lounge on the big overstuffed sofa that had seen a long string of better days. Then I came home. The couch—with its broken springs and loose pillows and the nickels and dimes and packs of gum and personal things slipped down in the cracks— stayed with me. It kinda reminded me of the old beat-up sofa we had at home, even dingy green, just like ours. Momma's antimacassars that she starched every other Saturday couldn't hide the age on that sofa at home.

My job didn't leave time for feeling bad or laying around on any kind of sofa. Not the next day after my lunch at Newboro, but the next Saturday, one of those hot humid days, so hot you wonder folks can exist at all, I stopped at a little shopping strip not far from Carver Homes. I needed a few things, sure, but I could have stopped dozens of places for bread and aspirin—little things like that. And got them cheaper somewhere else. That I stopped where I did, at a strip I'd been in only once before, made it seem the Lord was using me. I feel I was sent there; well, I feel that way now. At the time, I just wanted to get home and get my stockings off.

I parked and started up to the grocery when I saw a young black boy on one of those small wooden platforms with roller skate wheels. Folks now have forgotten what they look like. Little platform, maybe two feet by one and a half, padded, and the wheels nailed on underneath. When I was a little girl we used to see old legless black beggars roll themselves along on those platforms. Seems like every time we went into Augusta when I was small, we saw one of those poor men. When I got a little closer, the boy on the platform called me.

"Miss Genie." His voice was filled with fear and hopelessness.

I knelt next to him. "I know you. You're Baltharzar, aren't you? Baltharzar King?"

"Yes'um," he sobbed.

I had some peppermints in my purse. I gave him some and asked, "Baltharzar, where are your new legs?"

Several months before we arranged for Baltharzar, who was born with just stubs below his trunk, to be fitted with artificial legs. Then his case worker had set up sessions to have him work with a therapist. I checked once, and the therapist said that Baltharzar, though below average in intelligence, was learning to use the legs well because he had a good sense of balance. Here he was without his legs.

"Where your new legs, honey?"

"Paw took 'em."

"Took them? What you mean? Haven't you learned to put them on yourself?"

"Yes'um." His eyes were frightened. He looked around as if something or someone might attack him.

"Let's roll over in the shade, Baltharzar, and I'll get us a nice Coke. Then you can tell me all about it."

The only shade was at the end of the strip near the dumpster. We rolled down there and I said, "Baltharzar, you stay right here while I get a Coke with lots of ice in it. You had anything to eat today?"

He shook his head back and forth. "No'm."

"Well I bet that Burger Bin across the street has a cheeseburger and fries with your name on it. Just sit tight and I'll be back."

I went in the whiskey store where Baltharzar had been begging. No one there claimed to have seen him. I asked to use the phone. I guessed Baltharzar's family had no phone, but if anyone was at the office I could get an address or possibly some information from the case worker's report. The phone rang in the Saturday stillness of an empty office. It was 4:00 on an August afternoon, and I felt I was hearing it ring at the other end, too. I went across to the Burger Bin and bought two Cokes, and a double cheese and fries for Baltharzar. Funny I should remember exactly what I bought, but I do, probably because of the way the child ate it. He was like a hungry dog.

"Baltharzar," I said, "I've tried to phone, and I can't find anyone. Do you know where your folks are?"

With the fear still very much in his eyes, he shook his head.

"Think hard, Baltharzar; we need to find them. Were they going out for groceries? Did they say anything about what they needed to do?"

He continued to shake his head while he licked the salt from the inside of the little package that held the fries.

"Baltharzar, can you show me how to get to your house?"

He stared at me blankly.

"Let's go, step by step, Baltharzar. Which way do you live?"

His look was so blank that I suddenly realized he'd

been brought to a strange place and dumped. I couldn't leave him. He was an easy target for anyone. Legless and not very bright, he would be sodomized and probably killed by midnight.

"Tell you what, Baltharzar," I said, pulling myself together. "You come with me and we'll figure out what to do. We'll be able to think better in a cool place. The car is down in front of the grocery. You stay here and I'll come right back for you."

"I kin roll." He sounded as if he didn't want to be left alone. He thought I would leave him, too. And I knew he needed to feel confident about something.

"All right. Let's roll, but be careful. This is Saturday afternoon traffic."

We moved out slowly, but Baltharzar was sure and steady in managing his little board. Although he was only ten or so, his upper arms were very strong and his fingers, pushing against the hot pavement, looked like those of an old man. I wanted to know how well he made simple decisions. "You want to ride in the front or the back, Baltharzar?"

"Back."

I opened the back door, and before I could help him, he put his hands on the seat and pulled himself up. Instead of giving the pleased look I hoped he would've, he stretched out across the seat. I put the board in and said, "You fixin' to take a nap?"

"No'm. Ain't nobody see me this away."

"All right," I said, getting in behind the wheel. "We have about a twenty-minute drive. We are going out

Beltline. Does Beltline mean anything to you? Do you think you could find your house from Beltline?"

"Beltline?" he repeated, his voice trailing off in a question.

When I pulled in my garage, I said, "Baltharzar, here we are. Do I ever have a surprise for you! I'm keeping two kittens for my great-niece this weekend, and you can play with them. They'll be glad for some extra attention. Now we have two steps into the kitchen. Want me to give you a hand?"

I opened the door. He dropped the board to the floor, lowered himself to it, and rolled the four or five feet to the steps. He slid off so he was sitting on the lower step, boosted himself to the next step and then over the threshold and into the kitchen. He pulled the board up beside him.

"That's great, Baltharzar; you manage very well. I bet you'd like to use the bathroom?"

"Yes'um."

"And I bet you have your own system," I said leading him down the hall. I opened the door to the bath and stepped aside.

He rolled in, lifted the top of the commode and pulled himself up. I left him, amazed at his agility.

Because I'd had to sign special papers to have the artificial legs made for Baltharzar, I thought I might still have some notes in the file by the phone. I went in the little bedroom I used as an office and started through the stacks of papers on the desk. I heard the toilet flush and then the tub run a little as if Baltharzar might be using the tub to wash his hands and face. Then I heard him rolling down the hall.

"Here I am, Baltharzar; in here. It's a little early for supper right after the cheeseburger. Is there anything you'd like to do?"

"Watch TV."

"Easy as anything. Follow me and we'll fix you right up."

In the living room he pulled himself up on the couch and waited for me to adjust the set. The kittens came out from hiding and I picked them up and, holding one in each hand, sat beside him. "Here are the kittens. Stroke them. See how soft they are. They may want to take a nap next to you."

He was interested and stroked the little heads with his big rough fingers. A tenderness I would never have expected come into his face.

"You take care of the cats and watch TV while I look for some things, OK?"

"OK," he said, seeming to relax a little.

I went back to the papers, some of which I'd stacked up for taking to the office. After looking for about ten minutes, I found Baltharzar's address, the name of his parents, and some information about the legs. I had to act, and finding the parents or maybe some tip about them was the first step. I went in the bedroom and changed clothes. I didn't want no purse where I was going. It would be an invitation to kill me, and to be safer—as much as I could at least—I strapped my little pistol under my loose jersey.

"Baltharzar, I'm going out to get your favorite food

for supper. You tell me what you want, and I'll bring it to you."

"Anything?" His eyes were wide with disbelief.

"Well, I can't catch a whale so I hope you don't want a whale steak tonight."

He laughed. It was a funny noise, like he didn't quite know how to do it.

"Tell me what you want."

"Pizza with sausage and those fishy things."

"Are fishy things anchovies?"

"Yeah, somethin' sound like that."

"You've got it. Now, Baltharzar, I'm going to close the blinds. You take care of the kittens and don't go to the door if anybody knocks. You just sit tight, and I'll be back soon as I can find your pizza." Both cats were sleeping on his little stubs and he was careful not to disturb them.

I knew I had precious little time so I drove to the apartment where Baltharzar's parents lived. I didn't have much chance of finding them, but I thought I'd find out something about them. And I was right. After I saw a for-rent sign at their door, I asked a man sitting on the steps in the hall what he knew. Buildings like that don't have resident managers or people in charge so you can get help. You ask questions however you can and piece together an answer.

Without showing any emotion, without feeling or judgment, that old man in the hall said, "Yeah. Gone. Said they was gonna hock them new legs and clear out. Boy's maw looked kinna scared, but the man say he knowed the fence and them legs was bucks. Then they was goin'. Da woman say she pin somethin' in the boy's clothes. Don't know, but they gone, lady. Said that boy wasn't worth nuttin' and gone."

I asked him if he knew who put up the for-rent sign. He didn't, but I knew I could do some tracing on that.

"Pay me, lady, I done told you what you come to find, ain't I?"

At the time I didn't know if the story was true, but I gave him the two dollars I stuck in my shirt pocket so's I could get out of the building. Driving faster than I should've, I got back close to my section where I picked up the pizza and hurried home. As I opened the door to the kitchen, I called to let Baltharzar know it was safe. Safety had to be new for him.

"Baltharzar, honey, look what we got for dinner. Just what you ordered—a big pizza with sausage and anchovies—those fishy things. And I have a big jar of sweet tea all ready for us. Let's cut some and we'll have a feast."

He looked at the pizza box like it was a treasure, but before moving he was careful to lift the sleeping kittens and put them down gently on the couch. All my training in all my years told me never to cry, but that moment with the cats I had to fight to hold back tears. Baltharzar had known only brutality, but from somewhere in his simple soul, a gentleness for those cats rose.

I wanted to handle him and do for him the way he was doing for the cats.

When he had stroked the kittens, he slipped off the couch onto his board. Rolling over the carpet was hard, but on the slick floor of the kitchen, he made one swipe with his arms and was at the table. He pulled himself up to the bench and waited.

"Darlin'," I said, as I took the big jar of tea out of the refrigerator, "here's some nice sweet tea. You want lemon in yours?"

He shook his head.

"Tell me about your favorite foods, honey. What you like beside pizza?"

I put ice in the tea and placed the glass and a plate before him. Then I put several slices of pizza on the plate.

He ate a slice, clearly enjoying it and then he said, "Spaghetti, I reckon, and rings. Fries."

He seemed to know only junk food, except the spaghetti might get by.

"What you like to do?" I knew he couldn't do much, but I wanted to learn all I could about him. "What you do?"

"Nuttin'. I can't do nuttin'. My paw say I can't do nuttin', that I ain't worth nuttin'." He looked as if he might cry, and I didn't want to ruin his pizza.

"Why, Baltharzar, you are very, very good at taking care of cats. In the little bit of time you've been here, you've shown you can take care of kitties as well as any one I ever saw."

He smiled an almost smile.

"You make the kitties happy. Just look at them. See, they've come in the kitchen to be with you."

He stroked them with his index finger scarred down the outside from all the years he had pushed himself along. I felt the difference—the smooth soft kitten below, the rough coarse skin above. I wondered if he could sense the difference, too, and then, from that, the care he wanted to give the cat and the way he'd been tossed out and abandoned.

"Cat can't help none, though. Cat nuttin'. I'm nuttin'," he repeated.

"You know, Baltharzar, we have to see ourselves as doin' all right in order to do well, to move forward." I said it, and I knew the theory of what I meant, but looking at his stumps and his scarred hands and listening to his jumbled language, I knew it wasn't so. I mean, not so, really. No matter what he thought about himself, the case against him was bigger than life.

"I seen lots of cats kilt," he said, as if musing on the subject.

"I know, darling. Finding homes for cats is hard." I saw all the children I hadn't been able to find homes for.

"I seen my real paw snap necks. He jes pick 'em up one by one and snap de neck, like a chicken. And once he throwed the cat, 'bout this size, to the big dog what come by. Jes throwed it and then laugh at the dog get that cat."

He told the tale in a flat, noncommittal voice. The action was just fact to be recorded.

"Baltharzar, look how pretty these kittens are. We wouldn't hurt them. You take very good care of them, and when my little niece comes by to get them, she'll thank you for making her kitties happy."

He kept staring at the cat fur.

"And Suebelle, she poison some cats; I seen her. And one time she put a mess of baby cats in a big metal garbage can, stuck the hose in, and drown them. I hear 'em thumping and making noise. Flopping all around when the water come up. But then she poison them others; they just go away. They don't have to face no big dogs. Don't have to face no water hose in no garbage can. They free. They just go away." He stopped stroking the cats and looked harder at them. "Go away?" He was certainly not telling them to leave; he seemed to be asking if they wanted to go away. "I wishes I could."

"Where do you want to go, Baltharzar?" I asked. "To the beach? You like to go for a ride in the country and see some big animals? Some cows and horses?"

"No'm." He hung his head.

"Try to tell me where you like to go."

"My grandma she tell me that we go to the Lord, that we go to the Lord and be free. You just go away, she say, and everything be good. She say I got legs there and walk good. She used to hug me and say that first she go away to God and then I go away. And then, we be happy. Me walkin' and us laughin'."

He began to rub his bent and calloused finger over the skull and down the spine of the striped cat. I understood. His grandmother had been the only gentleness he'd known and he was trying to remember what she'd done for him, so he could do it for the cats.

"Where does your granny live, Baltharzar?"

"Gone away."

"To the Lord?" I asked. He used "gone away" in so many different ways I wasn't sure.

"Yeah. Gone away. I wants to go away. Then I have

legs and walks. Then I be somethin'. My granny say I would be somethin' with the Lord. My paw jes say I'm nuttin' and not worth nuttin'. I ain't nuttin', Miss Genie. Nuttin'."

I couldn't contradict him. To the Lord he was something, if all the things my father believed in and said were true, but here he was nothing. Taking his artificial legs to fence for a little money. Tossing him out in a strange place. Just tossing him out the way some people did litters of cats and dogs. Even telling a child that he was worthless. All of it was wrong, bad as a person could do. I could arrange for a new set of legs, but the legs seemed a mighty little part of the mess Baltharzar was in.

"Tell about your granny, Baltharzar."

"I stay with her when I a little boy. She push me 'round in the buggy from the grocery sto'. She rock me." He began very slightly to rock the cats. The motion seemed to be unconscious.

"She fix good things. Puddin'. She make this nice kinda yellow-looking puddin'. Then she go away. And I stay with my maw and new paw. He tell me I not worth nuttin'. Take my legs."

Baltharzar confirmed what the man in the hall said. The stepfather had taken the prosthetics. But Baltharzar didn't cry. He didn't look as if he wanted to. He was beyond tears, I realized. He'd gone over into an almost comatose state. At ten, his feelings were atrophied. At ten, he had the prospects and the values of a man of seventy waiting out the days of a life term in prison. Baltharzar was a child and a breathing corpse at the same time.

"Nuttin'. And when you nuttin', you wants to go 'way and be somethin'."

I had seen the reports on Baltharzar and knew his ability to learn was limited, that he was badly dyslexic and could learn very little by reading if he could be trained to read at all, but from his comments I knew he'd learned from watching and feeling. He'd bypassed the psychology and sociology books, the studies on suffering and meaning, all the treatises on stages of guilt and awareness and reactions to death. He'd missed all of this and gone straight to a vein of dark truth that the writers of Lamentations and Job understood.

"Them kitties what was poisoned and jes go away was somethin'."

Was it possible to change his self-concept? Of course I thought about it every day at work; and every evening when I slipped in, Baltharzar would say the same thing about being nuttin'. I tried to help.

"Baltharzar, honey, any messages on the phone machine? Did the phone ring?"

"Yes'um."

"Tell me the messages. You can hear them when they come in. You hear them as the machine records 'em. You tell me, and that way I won't have to play the tape." I wanted to help him develop his skill in listening and telling. He was silent.

"Please, Baltharzar, help me."

"Can't tell nuttin'. I'm nuttin. Jes like my step-paw say. He say I can't do nuttin'."

"You could help me with the phone."

Or I might ask him to find something. He would do physical things. He'd roll past the lower cabinets in the kitchen and reach pots I pointed out, but if I asked him to bring the biggest pot, he would say something about being nuttin'. I realized he couldn't judge size or at least he was afraid to make a choice. I'm sure he'd been beaten for bringing the wrong thing or being in the wrong place.

After my niece came for the cats, he thought the cats had been killed or gone away, even though he saw her take them away with a great display of love and attention. He started over on his recital of all the cats he'd seen killed and how much he wanted to go away to his granny so he wouldn't be nuttin'.

Well, the Lord moves in mysterious ways. Baltharzar had been with me over two weeks, but with care and food and love and attention he seemed only to hate life more. I think I reminded him of his grandmother, and all he wanted was to go to her and be something with her.

One evening I remember so well, I come home, fixed us a little light supper because it was too hot to cook, too hot to eat much, and sat down across the table from Baltharzar.

He barely picked at his food.

"Baltharzar, honey, what's wrong? You don't like 'tater salad and sliced turkey? Want me to put together a turkey sandwich for you?"

He didn't answer.

"Can't you tell me, darlin', what's wrong? Please."

He looked miserable, but all he muttered was "He beat me and say I nuttin'."

"That's all over, darlin'. You with me now."

"I seen somethin' today."

I was frightened. I thought he meant people had come for him, or he'd seen his mother and stepfather through a window, but I didn't want to plant any ideas.

"You see somethin' on TV, Baltharzar?"

"Yes'um."

"On TV?"

He nodded.

"What you see?"

"Some man jes quit eatin' and he 'lowed to go away. Like them kitties what was poisoned and jes go away. They all be free. They be something new. He jes quit eatin'."

He started crying. It was the first time I'd seen him cry, but he sobbed slowly and desperately. I moved next to him and put my arm around him. He kept on crying, inconsolably.

Finally exhausted, he stopped. And then he gasped out, "Miss Genie, why come I can't go away and be somethin'?"

I knew he didn't have the ability to make rational and informed decisions, but I also knew how meager the best of futures would be for him. I asked, "Baltharzar, what you mean when you say *go away*?"

He snuffled and gave a little moaning sound. "It mean walkin' free."

I held him to me. He had little strength left.

"Baltharzar, honey." I paused. I didn't know what to say next. Then like somebody put a word in my mouth and made me say it, I asked, "You know how to take a pill?

You know, a little round ball you swallow and then you drink some water to wash it down?"

He nodded. And I continued, "You can put a pill in your mouth and swallow it with water?"

"Yes'um."

"Did you take any pills at the clinic?"

He shrugged a little.

"Try to remember, honey. Do you remember putting a little round hard thing in your mouth and then the lady in the white gave you some water and told you to drink a little and swallow?"

"Yes'um," he mumbled very softly.

But I didn't have any pills. I couldn't ask anyone for drugs. That made a trail. My office had a supply, but by my own rule they were released only to certain people, and two observers had to watch the transfer and sign the book. I had made sure the room with the drugs required two keys, the master key and the one other. I had the master key. Even if my doctor would prescribe something for me, that too would make a trail. I had to be able to find or buy Baltharzar's new kind of legs without anyone asking any questions. And whatever I found had to be quick and painless so Baltharzar wouldn't feel his insides torn the way his spirit was torn. I wanted him to slip away as easily as his fingers had slipped down the back of the sleeping kittens. I wanted to be his granny's agent and help him. To end the heavy burden, and to let the oppressed go free. It was Isaiah, I thought, but I wasn't sure.

I watched him silently. He sat with his head down, a still life of no life. Other people organized to give fatally ill children what they wanted most—an early Christmas, a visit from a special person, a trip to Disney World. I had to organize to give my fatally living child what he wanted most. A trip to Disney World would have been easier; a trip to the moon seemed easier at that point.

I put my arm around Baltharzar. "Honey, I'll take care of you. I can't be your granny, but I love you the way she did. Try to understand that, dear. You're my dear, dear boy. I love you very special. I want you to be happy. I want that most of all."

His rough hand took mine.

We went on. No matter what I did, Baltharzar could not rally. And then something came to me one Saturday. Just came. I was vacuuming the cushions in my sofa and I thought about all the stuff that had fallen between the cushions of that old rat-trap of a sofa in the lounge at Newboro State. It wouldn't be impossible that a vial of pills would be there. Course, it wouldn't be too likely either. Too much of a coincidence. Like some great hand reached in and put it there just when I needed it. So I set up a promise to myself. I'd go look under the cushions, and if something was there I'd take it as a sign, maybe a sign from my daddy, certainly from his God. If there was nothing there, I'd turn Baltharzar over to state custody right away and pay so he could go to one of the private places and receive a little better treatment. I went in the lounge at Newboro early in the morning before any faculty members would likely be there. Quickly I pulled out a cushion, felt in the cracks, examined splits in the cording. Then the center pillow; then the third. Combs, a tampon, two quarters, the ring from a can of pop, a plastic straw, two movie stubs, a pen without a cap, an address book, a lipstick. The old sofa was like a smelly drugstore. I put all the cushions back and started out knowing that when I got to Manchester, I had to take Baltharzar to the office for custody and processing. Being nuttin' took on new meaning, nothing with a number.

But I couldn't stop thinking about that smelly old couch.

Even in the best institution we could place Baltharzar, he'd fall through the cracks. He'd be like the comb or the pen with no cap. He'd fall through the cracks in the system and hang on like a piece of lint down where the things we don't care about settle. I could see him, his half-a-body easy to fit in the cracks of a big sofa made of brick and concrete with maybe a marble strip around it like the cording on the sofa in the lounge. No matter what I did for the next week, Baltharzar in the cracks of my sofa moved in front of me.

I'd made my solemn promise to myself. If nothing was under the cushions at Newboro, I'd follow the steps my office enforced, but every time I picked up the form to start the proceedings, there was a sofa on my desk, and in the sofa was my baby. And I'd promised him I'd take care of him. Baltharzar was between the cracks, and I was between my promises. So I was back to what my family teased me about: Doing Right Hold Steady. Right then, two rights were holding.

Down the hall from my office was what I needed in the drug cabinet. But my rules for Children's Services held steady, too. And life on the street held steady. Folks on the street could get just what I wanted, charge me, and forget the whole thing. I didn't like it. Involving another person wasn't right. But when you're between the cracks of right, you got to do some choosing. I found a young man I'd helped a couple of times. "Sure, Miss Genie," he said. "Easy as anything. Nothing to it. You done a lot for me back with that probation officer."

Easy as anything. That was a lie. It was the hardest thing I'd done up to that point. But my bottle of Valium came the next day. It was plenty big for Baltharzar, but, all the same, small enough to slide out of a purse and get lost in any old sofa.

Baltharzar did little but sit and look into space. He'd stopped watching TV, and he said over and over in a little chant: "Go away and be somethin'; go away and walk free." I asked him several times every evening what he thought his granny would want him to do. He'd say the same thing, and each time it was like his voice come from off somewhere he was stuck in a lost dark place.

"Baltharzar, honey, you're all tired out. Here, lie down on the couch, and I'm gonna bring you some pills and a big glass of water. I want you to take all the pills. A pill and a big swallow, a pill and a big swallow, over and over until you finish. Will you do that for me?"

"Yes'um."

I carried him to the couch and fixed his favorite pillow behind him so he was upright enough to drink easily. Then I went for the pills and the big tumbler I used for iced tea on very hot days. I pulled up a chair by the couch

and, handing Baltharzar the big glass, I removed the top
from the vial and handed him a Valium. He put it in his
mouth, drank some water, and swallowed. I handed him
another. He put it in his mouth, drank some water, and
swallowed. And another. We must have looked like part of
a strange mechanical process with the same movements
repeated over and over. He slipped down and went to
sleep. He did not wake up.

Hours later, I brought out my old Sunday school
Bible, and found a passage my father used to read to us. In
Matthew 17:26, "Jesus said unto Peter then are the children free." I remembered another verse I thought was
from Psalms, but my little Bible didn't have a concordance
so I couldn't check. What came back was "free among the
dead." I put them together: "Jesus said unto Peter, then are
the children free, free among the dead."

I was not sentimental, but I hoped Baltharzar was
walking with his granny, and they both knew the glory of
being something—together.

The ground in the garden was hard for digging because it was another dry August, but there was a spot just
right for Baltharzar. I knew for him I had to have a tree, a
tree with very strong limbs to make up for Baltharzar's legs
and a fruit-bearing tree so there would be evidence of the
tree's efforts. Not a crop, just a symbol. I liked the idea of
a flowering quince, but that wasn't a tree, and, besides, it
needed the fence for support. I wanted a good tree that
bringeth forth good fruit, one that could be slender,
strong, and free-standing.

I settled on a pear tree and bought one that was

already ten feet high. Gus delivered it for me from the nursery, and I made him a batch of my special divinity fudge that he said no one else could make just right. Then I had to break the law to keep the tree watered. That was the summer we had the tight water ban. I used to get up at 2 A.M. and let the water soak into Baltharzar's pear tree until 4 A.M., when I went back out and cut the water off. There early in the dark morning, with everything still peaceful and cool, the damp ground and moist leaves glistened, and little rivulets ran sideways to other spots in the garden. Every morning I felt I had come to worship. "I come into my garden as a garden of herbs. My beloved is gone down into the garden." How lovely the language was as my father's voice intoned to me in the predawn stillness. Times joined and we were all together again. Every morning I sat on the bench in front of the azaleas, prayed to the God of love I thought for years I had lost, and then said softly to the black skin of night around me: "And he shall be like a tree planted by the river of water, that bringeth forth his fruit in his season; his leaves also shall not wither; and whatsoever he doeth shall prosper." All this is true because Baltharzar is something, not nothing.

I burned the little rolling platform on a Saturday morning and stood over its flames with the water hose in readiness so that no harm could come of the burning.

"Yes, thank you, that's all the lunch I want. Yes, I'm writing a little. Not much else I can do." That's all I said to the attendant. Seems that's all I've said to anyone in days.

The Lord knew when it was the weekend or Christmas or my vacation. He found the time for me to do His work. I wanted to take a few days off in October, and I had lots of vacation days saved up. Because of my daddy's teaching I never thought of vacation without thinking of vocation. He was an old black country preacher without much formal school, but he knew about vocation, and he had one. At the time I probably didn't understand, but now when I look back, I know my father was called to serve the Lord. And slowly I felt I was too, but in a different way. By 1980 I'd read everything Dr. King had written, and I use to wonder what he'd think of my choices. I never eased suffering with violence. I did make the children free. Really free at last. I served. I served my people and my God.

Like Enamel Toney. Folks couldn't pronounce his name. I was the only person who caught on to say it right, the way his mama intended with the accent on the first syllable and the last, and the *na* in the middle disappearing into a little *nuh* sound. Other folks, seeing the word, thought of a kind of shiny paint, but I always said *"Enamel"* so's he'd have a name that was his own. He didn't have a thing else. So, it was the kind of name that causes giggles and some meanness in school? Little Enamel he didn't have to face a room of thirty teasing children. Nor did he have to go through those gray-green corridors smelling of last week's soup, corridors filled with kids who laugh and point.

Enamel was born brain damaged, afflicted with cere-
bral palsy, and visually impaired. I use the professional
term that is not supposed to carry the stigma or connota-
tion that "blind" does. His mother, we all knew at the
clinic, had been on drugs during her pregnancy, and when
Enamel was born he should have died. And he would have
before the advent of newfangled medical means for fool-
ing nature. Technology and some ill-founded principle
saved Enamel, a child who never saw or gained coordination or learned to speak.

He made one sound, not nearly so odd as his funny
name. One little sound that sounded like "see" or "sea"
was the only thing that ever come out of his mouth. Less
than what a dog or cat can say.

What I did for my favorite boy child Enamel was both
hard and easy, and that time I knew the Lord was speaking
to me and through me. "See," the baby'd whisper to me;
"see, see." At first I had the impulse to look around when
he made the sound; then I felt he might be like an infant
Samuel, a prophet who wanted me to understand more
clearly. *See* in the big sense, all the dark stuff. "See,"
Enamel kept telling me. So I looked at him and the records
our office had of him and at his mother and at all his
siblings, not one who promised much, or—and I have to
add this—had been promised much by time or place or
biology or whatever. See, Enamel reminded me; see what
has happened.

Lots of times I wondered what Dr. King would have
said and felt if Enamel had whispered *see* to him. I know
Dr. King wouldn't give up the cause, but Enamel did

make you think it was all hopeless. Dr. King could have thought through this and figured it out and put it in great words. I kinda know, but I can't quite put it all together.

Leastways, I'm glad Stokley never heard Enamel whisper *See*. Stokley would've burned the whole works down. To Stokley, *See* would've come out "Git back, git even."

Well, anyway, Enamel stayed with me. No, Enamel did more than that. Enamel taught me to see. So we were all working in our way. Dr. King was dead, but he'd worked in his way to ease the burden. Stokley worked in his way. They had power or made power. I know that I really was making a difference. I kept some of my people from suffering. Enamel made me see that what I'd been doing was not a wrong thing. *See*, he told me, and I did see.

Enamel remained like some warm soft little creature that snuggled up and held on. His little arms held like he was a koala bear—you know that funny kind that clings to its mama. Anyways, he hung on to me while I had him. And seems the Lord wanted me to have him. This one was the Lord's work.

I knew about Enamel—we all did—for maybe three years and I tried to get him to the custody of the state. But his mama say she want him. One Thursday during the first week of October, still hot, still real hot, I go personally to see his mama about the difficulties the caseworker was reporting, and Uzella, his mama, felt right bad that day. She kept moaning about how bad she felt and that her man left her, so I asked, "Why don't you let me take care of Enamel till you get back on your feet?" She didn't object. That was Thursday. I said I would bring the little boy back on the following Monday. She just nodded like she didn't care what was going on. Nobody else was there. And I wanted to have Enamel tested by some new methods, and I wanted to love him. Wanted to make over and fondle him, give him the pats and snuggles nobody else gave him but that he could ~~understand~~. Then, I swear to God, I had no other plans. Ahead of time I never did. Everything I did was what seemed best of the possibilities.

I left Uzella Toney's house about three in the afternoon; the temperature was about eighty-six. I mean for October it was hot. I remember the day real clear because I was set for a two-week vacation beginning the next day and running till the Wednesday next after. It was the first real vacation I'd ever planned, but when I saw little Enamel, I knew what I wanted to do was give myself to him and give my time to make his time a little better. Not much. Wasn't much anybody could do. Just the pats and snuggles, just the pats and snuggles. I figured if I could just give that boy a few days it'd be the best vacation for me.

Now, you see, nobody but his mama knew that Enamel was with me. And Lord love us, the next day, she died. There I was, on vacation that Friday, sitting on my floor trying to make Enamel laugh and trying to work with his legs to see if maybe he had enough coordination to crawl. Well, the phone rings and it's my office saying that a police report just came through. Seems one of the older children came in late and found Uzella. He went to the old lady in another apartment. Nobody had a phone so she sent the boy out to find a policeman. Finally, things worked around and a call went through to Children's

Services since we were on the record. So on Friday after-noon I learned Uzella was dead, and there I was with her boy kind of gurgling and kind of smiling and off and on saying something that sounded like "See, see, see," and nobody knew he was there.

The Lord moves in mysterious ways his wonders to perform. Little Enamel could go into an institution that would care for him; he was free from the long neglect and casual indifference he'd known for the four years of his life. "See," he told me, like some old prophet. "See. See."

We spent the weekend rolling on the rug and playing.

"Enamel, cat, rat, bat," I'd say.

"See, see."

"House, mouse."

"See, see."

I tried all the sounds by themselves and in little singsong rhymes, but he couldn't reproduce any of them. He couldn't clap or crawl any more than he could see or reason. He could hold on to me; apparently he could hold on to life since for all his misfortunes, his little heart pumped along.

"See, see." What was it he wanted me to see? By then I felt the Lord was using Enamel to help me see something. Just like my daddy always told me.

Well, like I say, I'd put in for vacation time. Now Enamel and me would go on a vacation together. I'd planned to go to Jekyll Island for a day or two. I'm no swimmer and I sure don't need no suntan, but like to walk on the beach and think.

What Enamel liked most was being held in front

against my breast. He'd put his little hands out and hold on to the blouse or tee-shirt. He liked the tee-shirts; he'd kind of wad them up in them little fists of his. I guess he like them best because they were soft. Well, I went out and bought one of those front carriers—you know, the kind like a kangaroo pouch, but higher. He couldn't see, of course, so the color of the carrier didn't make no difference, but I bought the brightest red I could find. What I wanted was one that'd look like enamel, you know, the paint. I liked the idea of enamel for Enamel.

Well, I put little Enamel in his red sack and everywhere I went, he went. He held on with those tiny hands, fixed his blind eyes on my face and told me at regular intervals, "See, see, see." I became more aware of everything around me because I felt I had to see for both of us. I looked; I tried to see below surfaces. I tried to see whatever it was this little boy wanted me to.

I remember my old teacher saying something about sight given by the gods. Maybe so. Because of Enamel, God let me see. That much is true.

So I took Enamel, my baby, my little love, to Jekyll for our vacation. We sat in the sand, me and Enamel. I sat with my legs apart so he could lean against me and feel the support of my legs. I wanted him to know the sand with its silky wet feel and also its dry and sticky and grainy feel. I don't know, but for some reason I thought feeling things, that sensation might enrich his little life. I wanted him to feel the sun, in that strange, different way it feels at the beach. And I wanted him to hear the ocean's roar. Why? I don't know. Since he couldn't see the waves and know they come only so far and stop, maybe hearing the waves was just frightening to him. Lord, the shouting that had gone on around him at home. The roaring and letting loose he'd heard. Maybe the waves were terrible to him, too, but if I made him suffer, even one minute, I'm sorry.

But I don't think he minded. Measuring is hard; answering is hard; filling in for him's hard. He couldn't speak and he couldn't see. But long as I held him, he seemed content. I moved him back and forth gently and chanted to him:

> Row, row, row your boat
> Gently down the stream.
> Merrily, merrily, merrily, merrily,
> Life is but a dream.

I don't know how many times I said it. I wasn't thinking. I was just making soft, patterned sounds that seemed to give Enamel pleasure as we rocked back and forth on the sand. But after I said the old rhyme, musta been a hundred times, I started thinking about it. What could Enamel know of merrily? What spread out ahead for him? Nothing seemed too merry. He wouldn't even have the few good times most everybody have growing up. Life is but a dream. It must seem that way to Enamel since he neither saw nor spoke. But we couldn't tell anything about the quality of the dream. To what could he row a boat? Nowhere. Nohow.

We sat in the sand and rocked and played and I sang. He couldn't form the word *row*. When I sprinkled sand on his legs, he said "See, see." I tried to help him say "Sand," but that sound was beyond him. And then, lolling there, worrying there, I began to understand the Lord's will. Why Enamel had come to me just at my vacation. Why I'd kept on with my plans and brought Enamel here. I finally heard what Enamel had been trying to tell me all along. It was "Sea, sea," *s-e-a*, not *s-e-e*. What he wanted was the sea.

I moved down to the edge of the water so that with each coming-in, the waves would lap against us. I sat in the same way so that Enamel could feel secure but also feel the water come up under him and the little ridges of sand form and reform. I felt what also I knew, the steady crumbling in the little ridges and rivulets. Each time the water receded from us, Enamel said in a brighter, happier way than I had ever heard him use before, "Sea, sea."

"Yes, Enamel, yes, my baby, that's the sea. The biggest thing there is other than God. Oh, my baby chile, I wish I could make you understan'. I love you so."

"Sea. Sea. Sea."

It was getting late and a strong breeze was blowing up, so I carried Enamel back to the motel. I had one of those rooms with a little kitchen area. I always try for a room like that so I don't have to dress up and go out for dinner by myself, but this time with Enamel, the kitchen was a big help. I could fix things for him and feed him. That night we had boiled shrimp. I cut up tiny little pieces for him and fed him. His little bird mouth would open and then he'd taste the shrimp. His whole face would change. Something reached him at last, some sensation got through. At the taste of the shrimp, he glowed and gurgled. He crowed, "Sea, Sea, Sea." It was all he had, all apparently he ever would have. I knew I could put Enamel in the halter and carry him into the sea. At the right time no one would see me, or if someone saw, no one would notice.

So my answer was clear. The morning came clear too, one of those days that folks love the beach, and I knew that very early it would be mighty crowded. So I had to be earlier. I put on my bathing suit and strapped Enamel into the bright red front halter against my breast. "Sea, sea, sea," he said.

"Yes, darlin'; it's the sea. What you hear out there's the sea."

"Sea." He said again just one time like he meant to stress it.

"Enamel, honey, you want the sea. Well, the sea want you, too. The Lord sometime gives folks what they ask for. And you been askin' for the sea for a long time now. Then you be free, my precious boy, then you be free."

"Sea, sea, sea," he burbled against my breast. He was warm and sleepy. The fingers curled in space and then settled against me.

I picked up the big pin I always used to fasten the room key to my suit. Then I remember, as if I'm watching myself do it, I bent my head and kissed the top of Enamel's sleeping head. We went out the door. I locked it and pinned the key to the bottom of Enamel's carrier. Then, feeling the purpose, I walked across the grassy area, through the dunes, and down to the smooth pale shore. There it was. The sea, just like Enamel always said. I wanted to commune with him awhile, feel his sleeping weight against me and, at the same time, feel the power of the Lord here in the open. My daddy come back to me then. He made me see the hand of the Lord spreading out and molding his world, smoothing out the sand, piling up the dunes, putting the sea oats just so.

There I was with Enamel held against me like it was my child about to be born. I looked down. The baby in the halter made me think of being pregnant. If I'd a smock on, I'd look pregnant. 'Cept a little old, I thought ruefully. I stroked Enamel's head. He slept unstirring against me. I loved him. And I thought of my father and loved him. A good old man who never turned bitter and who loved the Lord whatever happened. And I thought of the Lord who made all this majesty and might. Who made heaven and earth. Enamel and Papa and the Lord God Almighty— they were with me as I walked along the early morning shore.

"Morning. You're out early." The woman spoke and startled me. I'd been so caught up in my thoughts that I hadn't seen her walking toward me, and on the sand she made no noise to break this blessed stillness.

"Good morning. Real peaceful, isn't it?"

"Real. That your grandchild?" she asked.

"Yes."

She moved over to look at him.

"He's afflicted." I volunteered so she wouldn't be shocked or embarrassed. "He can't see and will never speak. He makes only one little sound, *sea*."

"Well, this is the perfect place to say that," she said rallying quickly and stroking Enamel's head.

Her quickness and tact impressed me. She was a white woman, probably in her fifties. She seemed very trim, like she did exercises all the time. But our eyes met, and we understood what a trouble it was to have Enamel's burden and to have to cope with the world.

"Yes," I went on. "This boy like the sea. We walk like this every mornin' and evenin', and I sit in the surf so's he can feel the water come up 'round him. He like that. A little light rise in his face."

"I walk every morning, too," she said.

"Good way to start the day. Well, nice to talk to you. Maybe we'll meet tomorrow."

"Maybe so," she said, starting off. "Have a good walk."

Me and Enamel kept going down the beach. I spotted a ramp near one of the new motels and determined that I would turn around at the ramp and go back near my motel for the walk into the sea. That way I wouldn't have so far to carry Enamel, just in case someone else, rising early, wanted to talk. I reached the turning point and turned. In the distance I could see two smokestacks, part of the old paper mill. And way, way out I could see a large ship, passing like a dignified ghost off to somewhere. Between me and the ship, three little shrimp boats were out, bobbing and dancing. I was glad to see them because of the way Enamel liked his little taste of shrimp the night before.

We walked back so the motel was on my left, maybe the distance of two city blocks away. I reckoned when the distance was one block, I'd walk slant-wise into the sea and move out to about my shoulders if nobody was around. If I had to, I could stoop in less water.

I moved into the surf. The feather ripples broke against my black legs. I watched the gray-green of the water, the white of the scud, and the shiny black skin meet. It pleased me. The swirls like fairy hands come up around my legs to my knees. I liked the feel of the water coming and going and all the little grains of sand rearranging themselves under my feet. Guess that sand didn't have something as heavy as me standing on it real often. Then as I moved on out real slow, slow as I could, I felt the water stroke my thigh and the crotch of my bathing suit. Struck me, for the first time in all my trips to the beach, that the sea might be kind of like a lover with very soft hands, stroking and stroking. Coming on, the gray-green, white-topped water rounded my stomach. It touched the key pinned to the bottom of Enamel's halter and then it touched Enamel's bottom. He stirred just a little. I stopped. I knew he enjoyed the feel of the water, warm and soft, rising around him. He settled back against me, apparently completely happy, as if all his needs had been met. The water came up to his waist, a little past mine. Two more steps and Enamel would find the sea he'd called for in his silent, dark time on God's earth. I put my hand on the back of his head and moved forward, lifting my feet as little as possible. I didn't want to stumble, and the water was strong at my breast. "You walkin' on the water, baby mine; you walkin' on the water like the Lord," I crooned very, very softly to him. The water touched the infant mouth and nose. Enamel twisted several times, not violently, but like a child turning in a bad dream. He did not struggle. Enamel was free.

I turned back toward land and moved quickly onto the sand. I walked back through the sand and between the dunes and across the grass, all the time holding Enamel's little head against me, while the water first streamed from us and then trickled down. It was 7:30 A.M. on a day the Lord had made for freedom. Praise be.

I sponged Enamel and then took a bath to wash us free of the salt. Washing, I felt I knew the sea better than I had before Enamel had been my guide. "Sea," he always told me; "sea."

I checked out, drove back to Manchester, went into my little house rejoicing, and changed my clothes. Then I surveyed my garden. It was probably 6:00 or 6:30 in the evening, a good time for looking at gardens because the evening peace has moved in.

Like a bulb coming up, the idea rose in me that I wanted and needed to do something very special for Enamel. Of all my sons I loved him most, I realized; and I knew he'd given me most. He made me see, and he had given me the sea. He had, maybe not entirely, but in great part, returned me to my God so that I felt the great hand creating and loving the earth in a way I hadn't felt it since I was a young girl.

All those years. I had to pull myself up, as we used to say, and make a career, and help my people, and do and make a difference. Just *do*, as my mother liked to say; and just doing was hard enough. In filling all those needs that mattered, that had to be—I didn't doubt that part—I had grown away from my faith, the one my father had given me. Enamel brought me back.

Enamel was the son who led and taught the mother. Out of the mouths of babes and sucklings hast thou ordained strength. With the others—Herez, Peter, Guaraldi, Baltharzar—I did something for them because I loved them and because I wanted to keep them from a time of suffering that couldn't regenerate. With them, though I really loved and cared for them, I now know I acted professionally. I know many folks would find that funny, even mad, but I knew it was professional.

With Enamel, there was the professional element. I can't put that aside, I know that. But with Enamel the gift of freedom was more personal; it came from a more richly flowing heart. He was my baby and he gave me not just the vision and the sea but a part of myself back. This heart, too, is like an ocean that sweeps in with great waves of love and then ebbs when everything crowds in mean or hostile. It ebbs, as if to protect its core by surrounding it with all the reserves it can find.

What should I do for Enamel as a little tribute to the gifts he'd given me? I continued to watch the garden as the evening drifted down upon it. In a week or two the time would change and all would be black by 5:00 or 5:30. And here in October was not the time for major planting except maybe trees, and Enamel was not a tree. What was Enamel Toney? A spring plant, but a perennial. This I knew. Enamel came back and back and back. Because he was of love and vision, he would keep rising. No one else would have found Enamel fresh and beautiful, but to me he was. He was a hosta lily. It came to me that what I should do was make a hosta garden for Enamel. I could take the shady place next to the house where nothing much seemed to grow and make it into a little hosta garden. I could lay Enamel there tomorrow and then mark off the area, move any plants that were in the way, and have the soil rich and ready. Then come spring I could put out all kinds of hostas—the ones with the solid deep green leaves, broad and smooth; the long thinner leaves with white edges like fine lace borders on a table cloth. Maybe a little fountain or one of those spouting frogs, close to the ground, so Enamel would have—if not the sea—at least some water very close to him all the time. Then every spring the hosta, green and fresh, would come up on their strong fleshy stalks. And in summer they'd remain, serene and lush, like a little tropical rain forest here in West End, to tell me of seeing and of the sea. Until frost, until just about this October time every year, the hosta and Enamel—healthy and thriving—would be with me. In the full dark now I could see the way the yard would look next summer. I believed the Lord would say it was good.

I stood up and knew that I'd get up real early the next morning and lay Enamel in the bosom of my family and his God, and then for the year, ready the tribute of perennial life to him. I locked my back door and slipped through the dark house, led by purpose.

It was time to take up my tulip bulbs anyway so I began that way. In the early morning light before anybody else in the neighborhood was much stirring, I dug out the bulbs in the area that was to be the hosta garden. Coming upon a bulb, I lifted it out carefully so I wouldn't tear the roots or shake all the dirt from it. I handled each like it was a very small and fragile version of Enamel.

Then when the bulbs were out I just kept on digging. On and on, deeper and deeper. The easy, rhythmic swing of the spade was reassuring. Shoveled out, the soil was like incense, pungent and aromatic. Too many drafts of it and I felt I'd be drunk with love of the rich dark soil. Way down deep the soil was very moist. I wouldn't have been surprised to find a great heart beating away in the core of earth.

When everything was right and ready, I went in and washed up a bit. Christenings, weddings, and funerals call for a cleaning. I wanted clean hands for the Lord's work. I picked up Enamel's body and lowered him into his place.

"Enamel, my bulb, my beloved bulb, I give you your place. You have given me vision and love. My bulb, my dear bulb."

I felt the tears streaming down my face.

"In the spring the hosta will spring up in a green bower for you. Their rich leaves will wave here and shade you. They will say, year after year, 'Enamel is free. Enamel is free. See. See. See.'"

Still weeping, I shoveled the sacramental dirt back in place. I'd planted the dear and precious bulb.

I gathered the tulip bulbs I'd put aside earlier. While the soil was loose I decided to go ahead and plant the early flowering Dutch bulbs I'd recently bought. They would make a blue and yellow border for the hosta bed. The Dutch bulbs would be the first to celebrate Enamel next

March; then the hosta would follow. I knew conventional wisdom said not to plant the Dutch bulbs till right at first frost, but today was the time for serving the earth. I had to measure by the warming love of Enamel, not the coming of the frost. And it was definitely chilly. Sitting there after my hot work of digging, I felt, brisk and chill, the light wind against me. Winter was blowing in. When I cleaned up I'd need to put on a sweater. But Enamel, holy and small, lying in the earth like a native bulb, was warm.

> My beloved is gone down into his garden, to the beds of spices, to feed in the gardens, and to gather lilies. I am my beloved, and my beloved's mine: he feedeth among the lilies.

It was the Song of Solomon. Years had disappeared since I last heard my father intone those lines. And now it was true. My beloved Enamel feedeth among the hosta lilies.

I would put the Dutch bulbs in, too. They would survive, and if their blooms were small the first spring, they would blaze out in bright banners of color for Enamel spring after spring after spring after that.

Day Four

That Tuesday morning I got to the office real early, barely light, just sort of first grayish. No time for anybody to be out. There, huddled on the front steps but way back up by the building so you couldn't see them unless you looked real hard and were practically up on them, were two little girls.

Lord, why you trying me again? I thought, but I said right away, "Good mornin', girls, you're up early." The smaller one—only three at the time—was sniffing and crying a little, but the older one—then five—looked at me hard and said, "We 'sposed to stay till you gets here. You Miss Genie?"

"Yes," I said, trying to recall if I'd seen them before. Right off I saw pinned on the front of their coats with big safety pins were their names. On the little girl was "Lajosie"; on the older, "Janeece." Their faces said they were sisters.

"Where yo' mother, girls?" I asked unlocking the door.

Janeece pushed her sister toward me, and the baby handed me a dirty paper. I took it but without reading,

98

said to them, "Come in, girls, you need to get warm. I bet I can find a place for you to lie down till your mother comes. Too early for little girls like you to be out. And I think I can find some milk and cookies. Like that?"

"Yes'um," Janeece said, her interest picking up.

I turned on the lights in the building and led the two children to the lounge. "Sit here, girls; I'll get two cartons of milk outa the machine." While I found the change and put it in the coin slot, Janeece looked at everything like she planned to memorize it. I gave them the cartons of milk and found a bag of pecan sandies in the cabinet. I didn't know who brought them, but I knew I could find out and pay her back. Taking care of the girls was my main job right then. As soon as I spread out the cookies on a paper towel, I opened the crumpled note. "Take care my girls. I try but cant." That was the whole message. No name. Nothing.

"What's yo' mother's name," I asked the older child.

"Mama," she said simply.

"What do other people call her? Friends, people who live 'round you?"

She shook her head.

"You've heard them call her something."

No response.

"Are you named for her? Her name Janeece, too?"

Janeece shook her head. "No'm."

"Janeece, if somebody met ya'll on the street, what name did the person use for yo' mama? You know. Hi, Mary, or Morning, Jane, that sort of name."

"We don't talk to nobody."

"What's your last name?"

"Janeece my name."

"Janeece what? My name is Eugenia Putman. All of us have two names, a first name and a last name. What's your last name, honey? Janeece what?" I forced myself to keep my voice soft and gentle, but inside I was so furious with their mother that it was probably a good thing I didn't know who she was.

Janeece looked down and then back at me confused and frightened. The look was too old for her. It had a pain and a twisted set of reasons and threats and needs too great for a five-year-old.

"All right, girls, eat your cookies. Stay in this room; I'll be right back. And I'll bring you some things to play with."

I'd gone in early because I was way behind in my work and needed bad to catch up before the demands of the day started, but needless to say, I spent the whole day trying to solve the mystery of Janeece and Lajosie. The local hospitals made a computer search of first names but couldn't find anyone named Lajosie, and the only Janeece with the spelling shown on the paper was a two-year-old. Homicide and missing persons were on alert for a woman who might be their mother. We made fingerprint records from the two papers that pinned the names on their coats and of the paper with the message. That wasn't much help because too many prints overlapped and smeared. In just one spot could the machine get a distinct print. We sent it out across the country. I made a game out of fingerprinting the girls and even taking their footprints so we could try to check that way, but by the end of the day we knew nothing more about the little girls than that their thread-bare coats were the only clothes they had. Beneath their coats they were naked.

We had an emergency supply of clothes for children, so we could dress them temporarily. Other things were a lot harder to handle than clothes.

I took them home. We had a good day-care right there in the center, one of the best in the state because of grants and the interns from local colleges, especially Banks and Ingram. The staff agreed with me that the girls were so frightened and confused with all the new things that had happened to them that day, that the fewer new things they had to deal with, the better. I felt they at least knew me, and some familiarity was better than no familiarity. With me they'd be safe. We had no way of knowing if anyone might be looking for these girls. I offered to take them home and bring them back to the day-care the next morning. They needed to be in a safe place, and they needed to learn basic things like washing their faces and keeping clean. The day-care could teach them those things, and anything would be a step in the right direction. We realized in the course of that first day, that these girls had apparently not even been exposed to the things most children pick up in their first two or three years. They could have been kept in a box for all the recognition they showed toward ordinary things around them. The good part was they didn't seem afraid of new things. Only questions about who they were and where they'd lived terrified them. But whatever they knew, Lajosie couldn't tell, and if Janeece could, she wouldn't. But we noticed right away that whatever Janeece saw, she remembered, and what she heard she could repeat verbatim, even hours later. I was probably the only one who caught it that first day, but her speech actually improved because she imitated the questions I asked her and the comments all of us made to her. Even if for the first five years of her life, she hadn't been exposed to any formal teaching, her aptitude for learning was high.

As soon as we were in my little house, I said, "Janeece, Lajosie, let's look around so you'll know where you are. You're my guests; I want you to feel at home." We walked around and I called each room by a name to identify it, and then I named objects in each room as we came to them, ordinary things like bed and dresser and tub. Lajosie was so tired and sleepy she didn't notice much, but Janeece looked at everything and said most of the words after me. She asked questions. When she saw the sewing machine, she wanted to know what it was. She looked at the spool of red thread on the spindle and with her finger traced its path down to the eye of the needle. She looked back from the little tail of thread coming out of the needle to the spool as if to make sure they really were connected. She looked at that thread the way some kids look at Christmas morning. When she saw several pairs of shoes in the closet, she wanted to know how many people lived here. Anything brightly colored, she wanted to touch, but I noticed she drew back unless I told her to go ahead and touch the towel or the bedspread or sleeves of blouses hanging in the closet. Seeing what she liked, I went to the bureau and took out two scarves—really loud ones that people had given me but I didn't wear because they didn't seem quite right for my size or the office.

"Here, girls," I said, tying the orange and green one in a big bow around Lajosie's neck, and the other, a fuchsia and purple one, pirate style around Janeece's head, "you need some bright colors and soft things of your own." I turned them to the mirror. They were enchanted. Such small things, but to the girls, the scarves, bright and shimmery, were magic. Some of the fear drained from their faces and a new brightness came up in their eyes.

We finished up in the kitchen. I said, "Now, girls. You've had a tour of my house. You've seen everything here. While I fix us a nice supper, I want you to tell me all about your house—where it is, how it looks, what's in it. Tell me so I can see it in my head. Would you do that for me? That way we would be even. We would've shared our homes."

They didn't respond, but Janeece looked very carefully at the colors in the kitchen wallpaper and at the design in the dishcloth.

"Janeece, you like that dishcloth?"

"Yes'um."

"Does it remind you of a dishcloth you liked at home?

No answer. I tried again. "Maybe you helped your mother do dishes?"

She moved and looked out the window by the table. "Out there real pretty," she said with appreciation. "I like that."

"Do you like gardens, Janeece?" I asked.

She nodded, not taking her eyes from the yard, just

beginning to green up with the first warmth of early March.

"You like to be in a garden?"

No answer.

"Do you play in a garden, honey; skip and jump rope? Things like that?"

"No'm."

"You just sit in the garden and look?" Then I had another idea. "You been to the park? Maybe with your kindergarten or Sunday school?" I wanted some connections with them and the world that gaped behind them. But the child had no answers. "Janeece, tell about where you live."

With a terrified look on her face, she turned from gazing out the window and mumbled, "We move aroun'. I don' know. We move a lot." She cast a quick, hard look at Lajosie. Janeece was so clearly miserable I didn't want to intensify her distress, so I took the dishcloth, folded it, and placed it on the table next to her.

"Kin I touch?" she asked. I nodded, and she unfolded it like some treasure. She spread it on the table and with her finger traced around the shape of the flowers and vines. Janeece had good eyes, showed good coordination, a love for color and nature, and an interest in patterns. That was all I knew, not much to go on. I knew many therapists urged that children be allowed to draw their dreams and experiences, and the tracing of the design in the towel gave me an idea. As soon as we finished a little supper of potato soup and tuna fish sandwiches, all I had at hand since I hadn't planned on guests, I went in my makeshift office and found a red pencil, a yellow highlighter, a blue felt-tip pen, and a pencil with very soft lead. I took maybe twenty sheets of blank computer paper and the various pens and put them on the kitchen table in front of Janeece.

"Here, Janeece, honey, you look like you might want to draw something. You and Lajosie draw a picture of your house. Maybe a big picture of something you like to do, of what you remember best. A game you like to play. A toy you like a lot. You draw some pictures while I clean up these dishes. Then we'll have a dish of ice cream for dessert." I had some chocolate ice cream in the freezer, but to my surprise neither child seemed to respond. In all my years, I'd never known a child who didn't brighten at the promise of ice cream. If Lajosie and Janeece had ever eaten ice cream, they certainly called it by another name. Scraping the dishes and putting them in the dishwasher, it occurred to me that maybe the girls had grown up with people who spoke only Spanish or some other language. Maybe their English was limited to a few words because they didn't use it regularly. My Spanish was as limited as their English, probably more so. I couldn't test the theory, but, I decided, first thing in the morning, I'd put our counselor who specialized in Hispanic families on the job.

Lajosie was making lines on the paper, the kinds of lines you'd expect of a three-year-old who had never handled pencils or crayons before. Then I looked at Janeece's sheet. She'd drawn the pig salt and pepper shakers, the ones Herez sent to market, and her drawing looked a lot like the pigs. The scale was off, but the pigs were recognizable. She'd drawn them with the soft black lead and filled one in with the yellow highlighter; the other, she dotted with the blue felt-pen. The colors and the contrast worked. On a second sheet she was copying the flowers from the dish cloth. Absorbed in her work, she seemed oblivious to me. I watched her for a minute or two, then started dishing up the ice cream. Lajosie watched me, nodding occasionally, her eyelids heavy, but Janeece kept on drawing.

"This ice cream is really good," I said slowly and deliberately, putting a dish and spoon in front of Lajosie and next to Janeece's work. Then I carefully folded napkins and put one to the left of each little bowl. I sat down by Lajosie so I could watch Janeece as I said, "Janeece, honey, put your drawing aside and let's eat this good ice cream."

She put the drawing aside reluctantly. I picked up my napkin and in fairly obvious fashion unfolded it and put it in my lap. Janeece imitated me gesture for gesture and then looked at Lajosie, who seemed to take all her cues from her sister. She followed the pattern with her napkin as well as she could manage. Then I picked up my spoon and dipped up one spoonful of ice cream. Janeece did the same. When Lajosie touched the cold she let out a little squeal, but Janeece said in imitation of me, "This ice cream is really good." I think my heart did stop with love.

The next morning I took Lajosie and Janeece with me. They'd be safe in the day-care at headquarters and would begin to learn some social skills. Anything they were exposed to would be helpful. That was back when we had a big grant for teaching at-risk children. We had a big staff so everybody got lots of individual attention. The girls didn't speak Spanish. That was about the only definite answer we reached that day.

On Friday morning, Polly Jones, who'd been keeping a close eye on them, came in the office to say that Janeece had learned all the colors, the concepts of up and down, near and far, past and present, left and right, and was teaching them to Lajosie, who held to a teddy bear as if she would never let go. Janeece had pointed to the letters around the top of the boards and learned each one. Polly wanted to know if I had special things planned for them to do next week.

"Polly," I said, "Janeece strikes me as precocious. What do you think?"

"She strikes me as a girl who is both five-year-old child and thirty-year-old woman at the same time. She knows things she's afraid to tell, can't tell, has been threatened not to tell. She knows to keep things hidden. Children don't normally know that."

"That's the way I see her, but I wanted to crosscheck. I thought I might be reading too much in. But I see her as extremely smart, too."

"Extremely. Lajosie is so small, it's hard to tell. She's been hurt; she may be somewhat disturbed, but she's used to doing anything her sister does."

"Polly, do we still have some unopened boxes of crayons, the big boxes with all the colors?"

"Yes, do you want me to get some?"

"Please. Since this is Friday, I thought I'd take puzzles and picture books and teddy bears home and do nothing else this weekend except play and teach and look and learn. Would you put together a box of things for me. Make a list, and I'll check them out. You can check them back in on Monday. I know it's state property," I added with a laugh.

"I'll do it. Do you want me to let Lajosie and Janeece watch me pack it, or do you want to surprise them?"

"I think I'll surprise them."

On the way home we stopped at the grocery. I put Lajosie in the buggy and told Janeece to stay with me and stop when I stopped. I hesitated to go in a store with them because I was dealing with the unknown. Traps were possible; all kinds of horrible things were possible, but I knew we could not hide forever. Janeece was adjusting so quickly, I knew she would want to be out exploring a larger world any day now, and whatever Janeece did, Lajosie did. I felt pretty certain, though, that someone from another area had left the girls and gone elsewhere, like the woman in the Kmart, who left little Peter. My hunch was that, at most, the connection with Manchester was someone who gave the mother my name. That first morning, Janeece said they were to wait for Miss Genie.

Going up and down the aisles took a long time because Janeece and Lajosie apparently had never seen a grocery store before and wanted to look at and ask about everything, but finally we left with many bags of things I didn't need for meals but the three of us needed to share.

I don't know when I've been happier—or more baffled—than I was that weekend. On Sunday afternoon, all three of us sat on the couch in the living room. We'd been practicing tying their new shoes and counting. Janeece was remarkable. She could count far better than most children her age, and she hadn't heard a number—as far as I could tell—until Wednesday or Thursday. Lajosie could get to six, a good start for a three-year-old.

I pulled a magazine over and opened it to a picture of a young woman with a child. "Janeece, tell me about this picture. What do you see?" She told me almost everything in the picture. "How does this lady look?" The description was right, and at that point I wasn't concerned with grammar. As soon as she finished describing the lady, I put the question I'd been building toward.

"Tell me how your mother looks?" I tried to talk in the present so that they might think their mama was coming back, but I couldn't keep it up. My hunch said mama was dead or long gone by now, and I'd start talking about her in the past even when I tried hard not to.

Janeece shrugged.

"Janeece, you see everything. You look and notice. You just described this lady and her little girl. Remember the way you described the puppy yesterday? The puppy we petted when we went for our walk? You saw that puppy once and you told me just the way he looked. The color on the tips of his ears and his paws. You told me he had one tiny white spot on the tip of his tail."

Janeece shrugged again. She would not make eye contact.

"Janeece," I asked, putting my arm around her, "did yo' mama tell you not to tell anyone how she looked? Did she ask you to do that? Did she make you promise?"

Janeece did not answer, but she refused to look at me. Little Lajosie looked at both of us, wide-eyed.

"Girls? Look at me. I'm very dark like coffee, maybe, or a Hershey bar." We'd bought Hershey bars Friday, and both girls thought they were food from heaven. "Was your mama my color? Would we match, say, the way, this pillow matches the pillow at the other end? I picked up the pillow nearer me and pointed to the one at the other end of the couch. "Janeece, reach that pillow for me, please." She handed it to me and I put the two side by side. "See, these two are the same color, the same shade? If your mama were next to me, would we match the way these two pillows do?"

Neither responded.

"But Janeece, you're very light, a beautiful tan color maybe like tea with lots of cream in it. Is yo' mother that color, too. Does she match you?"

No response.

"Janeece, you know Ms. Bradley in the office? The lady who runs the big computer?" Janeece was fascinated with all the machines in the office. She'd sat next to Viv Bradley several hours and just watched what she did. "You know Ms. Bradley is very pale, with blond hair and blue eyes. She is pale like a piece of paper, almost, or your new cream tights. Was your mother closer to that color?" If I could find out if the mother was a white woman or a black woman, I would have a little to go on.

Nothing.

"Lajosie," I asked. "Will you tell me?"

Lajosie clouded over as if she might cry again. "Tell

you what, my pet. We'll use Janeece's crayons and we'll make marks on a nice new piece of paper. When you see a mark the color of your mother's skin, will you point it out?" Lajosie did not respond; neither did Janeece.

"Janeece, would you please get your crayons and a nice big clean sheet of paper?"

She didn't want to, but she stirred and crossed the room for them. She wanted to please me, wanted to do whatever she had to do to stay. By herself, she thought of getting a book to press on. She came back and sat by me again.

"Now, Janeece. Please start with the darkest color in your box. Make a nice wide line on this side of the paper." I pointed to the right-hand side. She took out the black crayon and marked.

"Now, Janeece, find a very, very dark brown and make a mark next to this one." She did. We kept working down the range of possible colors. And I even allowed for an Indian mama or Chinese, although the girls' faces wouldn't support the possibility. We worked down to the pale, pale cream crayon, a color that did look a lot like Viv Bradley.

I picked up the paper and rolled it back. I put the dark brown spot of color next to my cheek. "See this is about my color." I felt kinda silly like I was Ms. Mary Kay herself. I rolled the sheet another way and put a light color next to Janeece's cheek. "And this is just about the pretty color of Janeece." Rolling maybe one shade darker, I put the paper next to Lajosie and said, "And this nice color— like that good mocha ice cream we had last night—just about matches my sweet Lajosie. See. There is a color for each one of us. Which color would we put by your mother's cheek? Who can find it first?"

Lajosie could not resist. She reached out and pointed to the same color I had put up by Janeece.

"This one? Lajosie? Why what a pretty mama! I bet you look just like her."

I looked at Janeece, whose face changed from anger at Lajosie to relief. She started to cry. It was the first time she had, although Lajosie cried a great deal of the time. Something broke in Janeece that minute.

"What is it, honey? Tell me. Did your mother make you promise never to tell what she looked like?" Tears covering her fine eyes, Janeece nodded her head. The little girl had to grow up far too fast and make all kinds of hard decisions and do things she had no way of understanding. I wondered what else she'd been forced to do. "Your mama was doing that to protect you. It was a way to keep you safe. You know that, don't you?" I asked. Not sure myself but knowing what I had to say to help them, I gave them a half truth. "Is this really the color, Janeece?" Her ability to match colors already amazed me. Just the slightest difference and she picked it out.

"Yes'um," she said. "That color. Like me. Almost just like me. But Lajosie"—she pointed at her little sister—"she look more like."

I passed the paper back to Janeece. I knew she wanted it. She went over the crayons to make sure that each one was back in the proper place by color. She had arranged them over and over since Friday night and always left them in her perfect order. While she was occupied, I said, "Now you could tell me how big yo' mama was. Real big lady like me? Big lady you have trouble getting around on the sidewalk or in the hall?" She gave me a little halfway smile but shook her head. "Tiny thin little lady like Miss May down the street?" May was an elderly woman who appeared emaciated. She lived two houses down and had stayed with the girls about two hours Thursday evening so I could go to a meeting. Janeece liked her because May told stories about her girlhood, and Janeece listened as long as May would talk. Janeece kept making swooping lines with the teal crayon, which she told me was her favorite color. The lines followed one another like the ribs in a peacock's tail, each one spaced right and smooth. I still had trouble believing a girl so young, who apparently hadn't used crayons or pencils before, could make lines like that, but I saw her do it every day. She always wanted to be drawing something. She wanted to live where her crayons were. "Thin as May?"

"No'm."

"A medium-sized lady, though? Maybe 'bout the size of Lon's wife? The lady next door who gave you the gingerbread? About that big?" Lon and his wife seemed charmed with the girls when we were in the garden Saturday morning.

She stood up and reached her hand up to a point above her head.

"That tall? About the size of Lon's wife and as tall as your hand?"

Janeece nodded. The mother appeared to be normal-sized, but I could not tell exactly how tall Janeece meant.

"Could she pick you up, Janeece," I asked, "or were you too big a girl?"

"She pick up Lajosie easy, but I too heavy for her. She try though."

"How she wear her hair?" I knew this wouldn't tell me much, but since Janeece was talking, I wanted to keep her going. "Can you show me on paper?"

Janeece made a teal shape for a face and drew some teal hair that could be any short style. Teal skin was about as reliable as anything else I had at that point.

"Was hers curly like yours, Janeece?" I asked.

"Yes'um."

So somewhere was a light-skinned black woman with real curly black hair. Right off I knew I wasn't eliminating a whole heap of folks.

Lajosie had a little birthmark on her leg, just a little spot darker than her skin, not quite the size of a dime. I pointed to it.

"Lajosie, did your mama have a pretty mark like that?"

Lajosie did not answer, but Janeece slowly nodded her head. "Where was the mark, Janeece?" She pointed to my left shoulder. "On this shoulder, Janeece, on the left shoulder?" She nodded. "Janeece, put your finger right on the spot and draw the shape of the mark." She extended her finger and made a little oval just above my collar bone. I took her hand before she could lower it and kissed it. She kind of shuddered and then threw herself against me.

"I want to stay with you. I want to stay here."

I hugged her and said, "Janeece, yo' mama may need

us to help her. You would want to help her, wouldn't you? You wouldn't want her to need something we could give her, would you?" But Janeece just kept sobbing.

Then she said, "Please let us stay with you. Let us stay with you, Mama-Genie."

Mama-Genie. The sound went though me like an electric shock. They'd been calling me Miss Genie, the way most of the children do. I'd heard Miss Genie so often that it had no special significance. I'd been Miss Genie for years. I'd never been Mama-Genie. I had a new name. I put an arm around both girls, and we rocked back and forth. "Girls, let's sing a little song. I'll sing a line; then you sing the line. When you know the words, we'll sing the lines together. Ready? Let's go: Twinkle, twinkle, little star." We sang it over and over. We sang it while we made up the sofa bed, while Janeece folded the towels and Lajosie the wash cloths as they came warm and fluffy from the dryer, while we fixed supper and put out our clothes for the next day, and took our baths. Lajosie and Janeece splashed about together and then, still singing about a little star, put on the new animal pajamas I'd bought for them. Each one had animal-head slippers, Lajosie, rabbits; and Janeece, little bears. They thought the slippers were the best things they'd ever seen. I tucked my girls into the sofa bed and kissed each one.

"Let us stay with you, Mama-Genie." Janeece said again after I kissed them. "We'll be good. We'll do whatever you say." And Lajosie echoed just, "Mama-Genie." She was more than half asleep by then.

I didn't sleep much. I kept tossing and turning and

listening out for the girls, but long about midnight I knew I'd do all I could to keep them with me. I'd make the room I used as an office into a bedroom those little girls would love. Pink or candy stripes or fairies or kittens—whatever they wanted. We'd work on it together. I knew I couldn't make up for their pasts or even hold back something in the future, but for a while I could create a safe little island. And I could certainly be designated the legal foster parent. I signed the forms for such arrangements every day; my top associate could sign for me. Then I went to sleep.

When we went to the center the next morning, we went as a family.

We had lots of days of going to the center where the girls learned about things and people, and I did my work and took every investigative approach I'd ever heard of to locate their mother. I wanted to find her, but finding her was the last thing I wanted. As Eugenia Putman, director, I went through all the steps, the channels, the procedures. As Mama-Genie, I admit I did not want to find her alive. I know it's a terrible thing to admit, but I didn't want to find her alive because I would have to follow the law and do what I could to reunite mother and children.

The girls had physical examinations and proved to be in good health; they saw a dentist, who found no problems; they had their eyes checked. Their vision was fine. About the worst thing that happened to them was at the weekly parties for all the birthday boys and girls at the center, they didn't understand why their birthdays weren't on the big month-by-month chart. No matter how I explained that we did not have accurate dates of birth, they didn't understand, and Janeece kept stubbornly saying she didn't want somebody else's birthday. She'd picked up that a birthday was a special individual thing that only the self had. "My birthday" already claimed powerful connotations for her.

She understood so much that sometimes being with her was unnerving.

But then one day, mid-June and well before noon, a report came through from Missing Persons. The report described the body of a black woman with light skin, of medium stature, and with an oval-shaped birth mark on her left shoulder. A reasonably clear picture came in the fax. I put everybody I could on the job of making calls and looking for leads. The Manchester police pulled out all the stops to find information and find it fast. Ten or twelve officers and the chief had met the girls and been charmed by them. Finding out something about them became a personal crusade, not just a professional duty, for about two dozen people in many different offices.

That evening, after dinner, Lajosie wanted to go straight to bed. She'd played hard outdoors most of the day and was practically asleep at the supper table. Janeece and I tucked her in one of the new twin beds, and she went to sleep on her candy-striped sheets holding a Pooh bear almost as large as she was.

"Janeece, let's go in the kitchen and talk just a minute. Bring your crayons if you want to." I knew she wanted to. If she could have done so without breaking them, she'd have taken them to bed with her the way Lajosie took the Pooh. We sat down at the table, and Janeece started drawing flowers. She looked up at me expectantly, her face alert, her eyes keen with intelligence.

"Janeece, I am going to ask you to do something very hard. Now, I want you to concentrate and tell me if you can remember something. I need your help so that a lot of people can do their jobs right. Her eyes showed just a little of the old fright and the old hiding, an expression I hadn't seen for months. Will you do that, Janeece? Will you do all you can to think back. Nothing is going to hurt you. Nothing is going to take you away. I would fight like a tiger to keep you with me." She and Lajosie liked the idea of fighting like a tiger. They used the expression often. She nodded but without enthusiasm.

"Have you ever met anyone named Patrice Wilson?" She looked at me hard. "Maybe a little girl who was called Patrice Wilson? Someone about your age?"

"No'm. Seems like I heard it, but I don't see nobody's face." Then she heard herself and said quickly. "I don't see a face."

She could correct her grammar without knowing what she was correcting, but she couldn't find her past.

"One more, Janeece, what about this name? Have you ever met a girl named Lurleen Wilson? Did you ever play with Lurleen Wilson? Smaller than you but maybe looked a little like you?"

"No'm."

I believed her. Her eyes would have told me if she was lying. "Now here comes the hard part, Janeece. I want to show you some pictures. If you've ever seen the person in the picture, tell me who it is." She liked games like this. I was always doing things to help both girls recognize, catch up, learn names of things. We'd bought or made flash cards for practically everything, and Janeece loved the challenge of identifying whatever she saw. To miss a card was serious to her. She had a strong need for success and the confirmation that success brought. I'd assembled ten pictures of women, some photographs of neighbors, ladies in the office, my sisters she'd met, and my niece Martha from Augusta, whom we had gone to see one weekend. But in the stack was a picture of the woman I believed to be her mother. I had to take the risk with Janeece in order to get positive identification.

We started down the stack. I held out the first one.

"That Miss May." She said, and then she volunteered, "She use to play the piano so's people could dance."

"That's a good idea, Janeece. Tell me something you know about each one."

She brightened immediately. She liked to show off how much she could remember. Already I knew that when she was in school we would have to have some serious talks about being too dominant in class. If she pointed to a problem it was conceit because of her gifts.

I showed her the next picture.

"That your niece Martha. She has a little girl not much older than me, but she know her birthday. Her name is Genia. She named for you." She flung the words out as if she had been waiting for a chance to show off.

We went through three more pictures. She identified each person and gave facts without hesitating. Then I handed her the picture taken from the homicide report that had come in, the picture of Laurelle Wilson.

Janeece looked at it, and her face froze. She looked at me with that hard X-ray look she sometimes had, the look now accusing me of terrible tricks. "Who is it, Janeece, you don't want to miss one." She kept staring at me and then without looking at the picture again, an answer—barely audible—tore out of her.

"Mama. My other mama. The one what said never to tell nobody." Unable to hold out, she started sobbing. I moved to her side of the table and held her to me until she'd cried herself out. Then, what seemed a very long time later, a new silence came in. She was not asleep, but she was quiet and seemingly at peace against me.

"Now, Janeece, I have some very good news for you. We have found a record of your birthday. In October you will have a big party on the 14th. The biggest party you want. You can start telling me the friends you want to invite and the presents you want. Oh, Janeece, you have a birthday. I'm as happy as you are that we can plan a big-big birthday party. You were born October 14, 1981. We'll put it on the chart at school tomorrow."

She didn't say anything, but she looked at me with quiet wonder. Her face said this was the first thing explained to her she didn't understand. How could she have not had a birthday yesterday, but have one today? I knew that tonight and maybe not for a long time, I wouldn't be able to make it clear.

"And the second piece of good news is that you and Lajosie will really be my little girls. I have the legal adoption papers ready. We'll start processing them immediately. You're my little girl, and I love you very much."

"I can stay here?" Her voice was up, quizzical but half afraid, too. I nodded.

"I wouldn't let you and Lajosie go anywhere else. I love you too much."

"I love you, Mama-Genie," she said, putting her arms around my neck and whispering in my ear.

We hugged for a moment, and then I said, "Janeece, do you want a bowl of cereal with a banana before you go to bed?"

"Please. I want to stay up with you."

"Let's have the cereal, and, tell you what, since Lajosie is already asleep, you can come in and sleep with me. We'll snuggle up. I'll be your Pooh bear. Your very big Pooh."

The confusion and anguish lifted from her face. She knew she was safe. I knew she'd weathered the crisis. What I feared might be extremely traumatic for her did not seem to have been.

What Janeece could not know then, although I wrote it all down so that she would have a record when she needed it later, was that she and her sister were the daughters of Laurelle Wilson, for whom we were never able to establish a husband, but then we were never able to establish much about her. Janeece had been born in Frederick, Oklahoma, and the hospital record said her name was Patrice Wilson. Lajosie was born in Perryton, Texas, and left the hospital with the name Lurleen Wilson. I concluded, and the specialists in such matters concluded, that Laurelle Wilson, who had many aliases, called the girls by different names so that tracing them or her would be difficult. She died from exposure near Wamblee, South Dakota, in March, not too long after we found the girls. We found a Social Security number and through that traced some waitressing jobs here and there all over the country. But no employer remembered her. She was one of the hundred faceless women who just pass through. I thanked God for all the big computer banks with names and numbers and fingerprints. You see, that one finger print we could take clean from the name pinned on Janeece's old coat finally matched a print on file for Laurelle Wilson, who once drove a stolen car. We learned nothing else. But twenty years ago, before the big data banks, we couldn't have learned this much.

Later when they were securely mine and we all felt the trust, I asked, "Girls, you remember yo' daddy?" But I never got any response. Neither one ever revealed anything about a father, and by then I knew them well enough to know they really didn't know anything about a man. He had to be white, I'm certain. And either Laurelle or the father of Janeece must have had remarkable genes for intellect and art. And Laurelle's face, even in the terrible picture of the corpse, could explain the beauty into which Lajosie gave every sign of growing.

Right after the conversation with Janeece and the identification of the picture, I pulled all the strings I had to get the adoption through in record time. The only question was my age, and because everything else was so right and the girls loved me so much, I think I could have gotten the age through, too. But just to be safe, I asked my niece Martha to sign the papers as a kind of backup. She agreed to be legal guardian, but she said she couldn't be mama. She was being nice, I knew. Didn't want to give the impression that she could be me. Martha is real thoughtful that way. She said she couldn't fill my shoes, and she made a big thing that Janeece was so smart and Lajosie so pretty that folks would be fighting for them. Laughing, she said she could auction them off to the highest bidder. Martha was in her early thirties and had children—Little Genie and a boy Ralph—close to the ages of my girls. With Martha's relative youth and my record of love and care, of responsibility and ability to provide stability and opportunity, the adoption went through faster than any I'd ever seen.

With her sixth birthday coming up October 14, Janeece was old enough to start school that fall. I fixed it so she would enter first grade at Banks Academy, but I wanted to have my own personal Head Start program to make up for those years when both girls missed so much. I arranged with students at Ingram and Banks to spend four hours every afternoon with the girls throughout August. College girls to take them around, correct their grammar, play word games, read to them all the stories children are supposed to hear. During the four hours there could be no television, but almost anything else to see and do was OK. One week we had white girls from Ingram College; the next, black ones from Banks College. Then both, together. My daughters had both races; I saw them as the future. I wanted to see to it that both white and black women helped get them ready for school. I wanted confident, independent young women, also of the future.

The girls I hired were perfect. And they did a good job, accomplishing more than I would have guessed they could in so short a time.

I pulled strings to get her in Banks Academy, but it wasn't too hard. Banks College thought of me as one of its distinguished graduates, as the folks there said. They'd have taken a dozen daughters for Banks Academy, if I had them. It was the best private school in the area—well, really second best—but the best I could afford and work out. With the other one, you practically had to be registered at birth and prove your grandfather paid a poll tax. No power on earth would have gotten the adopted mixed-blood child in the very best school even though her first test scores were in the top one percentile.

Banks was just fine for us, though. People, like plants, have to have roots or they wither. I just had to make sure Janeece was ready. She couldn't deal with failure or even being second.

But what I remember best, what I like to think back on and picture in my head is the night before she started school. It was Labor Day, and Alma Faye and Gus were still at the house with us. Since Banks was a private school, classes started the next day. Janeece fretted the week before because her little friends in the neighborhood started the public schools, and she felt left out. My niece Martha and her family had headed back to Augusta; they had to see about getting their two children ready to go back to school after the long weekend. We'd had pickup supper, and the three adults were sitting on the porch. Jan and Josie, as I now called them, were in the yard, playing they were fairies in the woods. They'd run and wave their arms like wings as they swept from bush to bush. It's surprising how quiet they were. The yard was like a stage set for a ballet, that stately kind, with all those green branches framing a moment and two dancers moving with a grace that seems to say gravity has been repealed and ugliness put on hold.

We sat there watching them, spellbound. Then Alma Faye said, "Genia, I never thought you'd let children run over yo' yard. You've sweated over it ever since you bought the house."

"Love changes things. What else can I say?" I replied without looking at her. "The garden is a joy, and a thing of beauty, but the girls are greater joy and greater beauty."

Then Gus, in a very serious voice, said, "I've been in this garden lots of times, visiting here and bringing bushes over. It's never been as fine looking as right now."

For Gus, this was a very emotional thing. His wife and I both reached over and patted his arm. "Thank you, Gus," I said, "I 'preciate that from you. You know gardens."

Just then the gas lights that come on automatically to light the garden glowed into the September night, and both girls paused in their fairy land. They showed shadowy and magical, as gauzy and soft as the place itself. Then Josie said, "Mama-Genie, look at the frog." She pointed to the little spouting frog in the hosta garden. We all looked. The sheen and angle of water and light, and the time of day, had turned the frog to gold. The figure sat poised and transformed, the common concrete of its shape forgotten in the deep gold tones of evening among the wet and dark and lush hosta lilies. We looked at the frog, transfixed.

Jan moved slowly to the bench and sat down in what she considered her new ladylike way copied from the college girls. "I love it here, in the garden. I come out when the sun is out and watch the sundial. It talks to me."

"That's a beautiful idea, Jan. Can you tell us what it says, or is it a secret?" I asked.

"What it tells me is hard to put in words, but it kinda says to move with the light."

We were silent. She had cut through to the secret of survival, this child who'd seemed destined for early ruin. She'd learned all she ever needed to know the day before her first day of school. There with the azaleas, the hollies, the gold-spotted aucuba, the hostas, the lovely butterfly bush, the Christmas rose, all the vines, and the hundreds of bulbs under the earth, now collecting their lives for next spring; there with a frog that seemed to be gold, spouting little cascades of gold water, Jan Putman told us the secret of survival.

Gus said softly, "Alma Faye, honey, we got to go. We got to move with the dark right now so's we can move with the light first thing in the morning." He opened his arms, and Jan and Josie ran to him. He'd become their father figure.

"Don't go, Uncle Gus. Don't go."

"Girls, I love you lots, but we got to go. Here, Jan, you get on my back, and then, Josie, I'll pick you up. I'll give you one last bookety-bookety ride around the garden, and then we got to go."

Holding both of them with ease, he moved all over the

yard, around and about and in and out of the bushes. As they approached the porch, Alma Faye and I heard Jan say, "Whoa." Gus let out an imitation whinny, and the girls giggled with delight. Anything Gus did, they thought was wonderful. He put Josie down and turned so Jan could step off on the top step.

"Thank you for the ride, Uncle Gus. Good night, Aunt Alma Faye. I enjoyed the chocolate cake and the salad. Josie did too." Jan made the speech without prompting, and when she nudged Josie, the little girl said, "Thank you, Aunt Alma Faye."

In the dim light, I could see tears shining in Gus's and Alma Faye's eyes; I felt tears in my eyes too.

"Thank you for letting us spend Labor Day with you," Alma Faye said. "Work hard in school."

"We'll see you soon, girls," Gus said, bending to kiss each one.

That was Labor Day 1987. But starting school was when everything changed.

I knew Josie felt kinda sad being separated from Jan and confused with all the attention her sister had received for the first day of school, so I called in and told my secretary I wouldn't be in the office till after lunch. I wanted to spend the morning with Josie and help her feel she was loved and had some special attention. She didn't have the interests and curiosity Jan did or we'd have gone to the Children's Museum or the botanical gardens, two of Jan's favorite places, but we went to the big toy store so Josie could pick out a new stuffed animal. Until she came to me, she'd never had one, and hugging a teddy bear or carrying her Pooh with her gave her a lot of comfort. Her bed was covered with animals, but she always wanted another one. I knew she was compensating for all the years of not having anything to snuggle up with, and I always tried to find a different creature. That way she could learn their names and we could read about where different animals lived. We went to the store and she looked at every soft and furry toy. I made her say which ones she already had. The process took a long time because Josie didn't like to concentrate. She wanted to jump around and touch everything. But we made a game of it and finally decided that the gray koala bear would be best. She held the bear against her and stroked it softly, cooing and making happy noises somewhere between words and sounds. Josie was a beautiful child with her striking coloring and big eyes. Holding the bear and loving it, she looked like a little model for children's clothes or Christmas toys. Between the stuffed-animals section and the check out, I saw a sales clerk I'd worked with in a girls' support group a couple of years ago. Rayona came up and hugged me and wanted to know who the beautiful little girl was. When I said that Josie was my adopted daughter, she was good enough to say that Josie had to be the luckiest little girl in the world. That was real nice of her, and Josie behaved just like I'd taught her to. She actually put out her little hand—four years old now—and said, "My name is Josie." I was so proud of her, I felt the whole world was fine and I could face anything.

Funny how things happen. That was the day I had to face something harder than I'd ever faced before. No explaining the funny way things happen. That was the day. When Josie and I left the toy store, it was 11:00 so I said, "Honey, let's stop at the Burger Bin and get lunch, then we can go to work and your school." I knew I had to remember to call the day-care "school" so Josie wouldn't think she was doing less or getting less than Jan.

"OK, Mama-Genie," she said getting in the car. I hooked her in the child-seat, and she sat in her prim way, smoothing her clothes just a little under the straps and then holding the koala bear very carefully. I could see her as a fashion model with her care for clothes and her good looks. She looked like she would grow up long and slim and graceful, all the things I wasn't. The difference amused me, but I was awful glad I'd have a good many years before I had to worry about her looks and her life. Why, her permanent teeth weren't in then.

We drove to the Burger Bin near the center, the one on Old Dixie Avenue and went in. Without being told, she left the new koala in the car. She never liked to get things soiled. She wanted a pure and antiseptic world with no spots. And small as she was, she had concluded that when she went to the Burger Bin, her fingers always got greasy.

Inside there were maybe eight people and four or five workers, some just behind the counter, the others behind the big racks in the middle of the work area. With us, there were probably fourteen people in the store, but, of course, I didn't count. I didn't know it mattered to know exactly how many people were in an ordinary Burger Bin at one time. Josie and I were looking up at the menu sign, and I was reading it off to her line by line, not just to help her choose what she wanted (we both knew what she would ask for) but to help her with her reading. When I said "Cheeseburger," a tall black man who'd just been handed his order in a Burger Bin bag by the girl at the counter, turned in a spin, opened fire, and shot all around that room. What happened is part of the public record now. The TV showed shots of the bodies for weeks. All I saw was Josie fall. I fell by her and cradled her under me so that if the man shot again he couldn't hit her. As I put my arm around her, I could see how much she was bleeding. How he could kill her with that tiny body so short it didn't reach the counter top and so slim she didn't have a sideways and miss my two hundred-plus-pound body I don't know, but he grazed my arm, just enough to shock me for a minute or two. He killed her with one shot. I came to instantly and heard the sirens coming. One of the workers in the back had stepped on the alarm and the police were on their way.

The police didn't catch him. The papers ran a headline about the Burger Bin Massacre. They talked a lot about Josie because she was the smallest and the most innocent of all the people there. Her little body was beautiful all embalmed and laid out in a pale pink casket. The funeral home asked for her favorite toy to put in her hands. I took her new koala.

DAY FIVE

The crowd was chanting and screaming in the street. One gigantic banner read: "How many, Travis?" Another, "What's in the Dumpster?" A third, "Dig Now." Under the posters and banners streaming in every direction, the television cameras and media trucks moved about and attempted to capture all corners.

When the anchor, sitting safely in the insulated silence of the newsroom, came on the screen, I knew what to expect. In his canned anchor diction with his sterile anchor speech pattern, he offered his explanation: "In September 1987, a cocaine addict standing in line at the Burger Bin on Old Dixie Avenue took his lunch bag from and paid the young woman at the cash register, turned, pulled a gun, and opened fire on midday customers and workers in the fast-food restaurant. Eight people, including a four-year-old girl, died. The gunman escaped and there were no leads and no tips for over a year. In February 1989, a drug dealer in a plea bargaining arrangement gave the name of Travis Mozell to law enforcement officers. An investigation followed immediately."

Next he talked about the search warrant that permitted officers to go into Mozell's room, where they found hundreds of the little salt, pepper, and catsup packages from the Burger Bin and hundreds of foil wrappers from burgers and fries. The room was knee-deep in wrappings from the place. Then he told of the discovery of seven-year-old Charlton Luther's body in the dumpster behind the Burger Bin on Old Dixie Avenue and the presence of six salt packets, three pepper packets, and two empty foil containers of catsup. In the pocket of his tee-shirt, his only clothing, was an elaborately folded and rakishly arranged napkin from Burger Bin. A similarly styled napkin was taped over his genitals like a new-style fig leaf.

Going only on the Burger Bin connection, officers put Travis Mozell under round-the-clock surveillance. The man went at least once a day to the Burger Bin on Old Dixie Avenue and several times a week to other Burger Bins in and around the city. He had no visible means of support, but he always bought a cheeseburger, a bag of fries, and a large drink. Before leaving, he always put a handful of the little condiment packages in his bag. He always paid, and he did nothing to call attention to himself. Hearing the manager of the Burger Bin on Old Dixie call Mozell by name, the officer, who was pretending to be a customer, stayed and, identifying himself, asked what the manager knew about Mozell. Mozell had once worked at that Burger Bin as counter help, but he claimed he owned the place—and acted like it. Fired for insubordination, he left screaming he would get even. But, as far as the manager knew, Mozell did nothing. He came in almost every day, bought his lunch, and left.

Next the TV anchor showed some clips of the body of Charlton Luther; then he ran the old clips of the bodies lying on the floor of the eatery. There was a shot of my darling Josie's face. Next he talked about the discovery of the body of Jingle Sprinkle in the woods about twenty yards from the dumpster of the Burger Bin in Olympia, thirty miles northwest of Manchester. Around Sprinkle's head, police found foil Burger Bin wrappers twisted and stapled together to form a crown. The boy's hands were in bags from the eatery, and, in the most gruesome gesture of all, sticks of French fries were stuck up his nostrils and anus. Over his clothes the boy wore the little orange and purple jacket of a Burger Bin employee. Several clips of Sprinkle flashed across the screen, capturing exactly the hue of the purple and orange, very little soiled from its time in or near the dumpster.

On the pattern of evidence from Burger Bin materials, the police arrested Travis Mozell. They showed pictures of him to all the survivors who'd been in the Burger Bin the day of the shooting, but no one could give absolutely sure identification, the anchor said. It had all happened so fast and everyone had been ducking for cover. A tall, thin black man was a commonplace in the Burger Bin on Old Dixie Avenue. There was no reason anyone should have remarked him. The anchor mentioned me and identified me as the director of Manchester's Office of Children's Services and the mother of little Josie Putman. He quoted me as saying, upon seeing the picture, "No, sir. I can't say anything stronger than that both men are tall, thin black men. That was what I saw that day; that is what I see today in your picture. I can't say it's the same man. I was on the floor, face down over my child."

Then Bosco Bullins, an activist with a bad reputation and a string of DUI arrests, got the idea that the boys reported missing in the preceding ten years were all victims of the Burger Bin Killer. He insisted that the city dig up all the landfills where Burger Bin dumpsters were unloaded. When the city said it could not dig up ten years of garbage, Bullins organized the rally.

I heard the smooth-tongued anchor say, "That's the background for tonight's Mothers' March for the Children."

The actions and gestures seemed stagey and the demonstrators as mechanical as robots. The TV trucks and all the whirring pieces of news technology were more faces of the mob. Police tried to keep a lid on. That night the city, expecting burnings in the housing projects, feared the negative publicity already rolling through the cameras, as the crowds assembled. The cameras were invitations to assault. Area buildings were boarded tightly, as if destruction had already occurred. It was the Mothers' Rally for the Children. Or in the street slang of the time, Dig-Our-Kids Night. For weeks advance publicity prepared for this. People were there from all over the world. It was a happening, one of those battle lines to which true believers and mercenaries flocked in equal numbers to see and to be seen, to feel and to give vent to feelings. The lights and noise spun and rose. Neon signs flickered and all the background street scenes showed up different from the

way they looked in real life. It was a stage set for glory and
death. Nothing was left of real feeling. The event already
gave off something of dead fish. It looked like the way a
too-old fish smells. But the promoters sure knew how to
work a crowd. Now I knew some of the mothers, poised at
that moment for instant stardom in this rally. I'd dealt
with most of them. I caught on right away how craftily the
rally was staged and how the mothers had been both
coached and paid with large sums for their grief.

Bosco Bullins, seemingly sober, led Molly Alexander
forward.

"Brothers and sisters," Bosco screamed into the mike.
"Brothers and sisters. We all cry the loss of our children,
but think of these mothers. They have lost their babies."

The crowd moaned out, "Lost their babies; lost their
babies," and Bosco resumed. "We want to hear these
mothers speak and we want the world to hear." He looked
at and gestured toward the TV cameras. "We want the
world to know that we won't take the stallin' and the
puttin' off any longer. Find the children. We say find the
children, now."

The crowd picked it up: "Find the children. Find the
children, now. Find the children. Find the children, now.
Now."

The marching about resumed. Bosco knew his tim-
ing. He let the crowd play its emotion just enough to help
his cause, then he reined in. "I say. We want action. We
want to find the children, now. I say we want to see these
mothers satisfied. Our mothers won't be crucified to keep
Manchester's garbage clean. We want justice for Herez

Alexander's mother, for Charlton's Luther's mother, for Jingle Sprinkle's mother, for Baltharzar King's mother. We want love and justice for them all.

"And though our sister Uzella Toney is no longer with us, we want justice for her. The Lord called Uzella Toney. Wanted her home to comfort her in her grief, wanted to stop her tears, tears for the little boy, her sweet son, she wouldn't see no mo'. Wanted Uzella home."

The crowd started up with "wanted her home," but Bosco broke in. "We won't have some ordeal like other cities. We care too much to lose what we love most. We care so much we want action now. We've lost five boys we know of; who knows how many more? Who know how many, wearing Burger Bin crowns, are layin' in the land fills like they was garbage. The Lord says we should not lose even one more, not one more precious little lamb of a child. We care for our babies, care so much that tonight we ax you to hear these mothers what lost their precious lambs, the babies they nursed, carried in their bellies, the babies they loved and cared for."

While he helped the weeping Molly Alexander to the microphone, I concluded again that the Lord must have worked overtime in finding Baltharzar King's mother to get her here tonight or in getting the message through to Uzella Toney to "call her home." Looking back I see it all so clearly now. What passed for mother love was fraud.

"Here is Molly Alexander, whose boy Herez, that she loved and cared for and gave up for, was taken from her. She don't know if he's alive or dead. But it's been many years now since he slept next to his mama's side. Here's little Herez's mama."

The crowd crooned, "Molly, Molly, Molly."

Cleaner and steadier than she'd ever been, Molly leaned heavily on Bosco as if she couldn't stand under her own power. She began in a staged whisper, "I kinda feel like there's no justice anywhere. Who do you go to for justice? Who can bring my baby back?"

"Bring her baby back; bring her baby back" rang out through the crowd.

Bosco patted Molly on the shoulder, as she resumed. "I give up everything to take care of my little Herez who wasn't quite right but what I love with all my heart. And he be taken from me. Nobody come and look for him. Nobody make no big search until it seem too late to do some good. If Herez be a white boy, a search been done long ago. Every dumpster at every Burger Bin be upside down long ago. We dig up the land fills fast if the lost boy was white. Dig up the land fills. Help me find my child." There she stopped, her face like she was trying to remember something. The line come to her. "Help me find my child so's I can love him; or if the Lord done called him, so's I can give him a church burial and do right by him. For love of Herez, help me find the justice."

The crowd went wild. "For love of Herez. For love of Herez" ran out through the streets in a great ascending chant. The cameras moved over the crowd, and reporters got ready to do face-to-face interviews. Then Bosco broke in again.

"Brothers and sisters. You hear what Molly Alexander—whose little Herez is like God's little lost lamb—say. Molly, do you have a last word for us?"

Throwing her arms straight down and slightly behind her and her face back, Molly cried out into the blur of lights, "A baby belong with his mama. A baby belong with his mama. That there's my baby, and he is took away."

She moved her arms forward, extended them reaching, and seemed to draw some invisible child to her and then up to her breast where she cradled him, rocking and sobbing. Her face, thrown back to catch the fall of the light, looked like all of suffering maternity. I thought right away of Mary when Christ was killed, and then, just as fast, of mothers in slavery who had their new babies torn from them and sold. And I hated Molly Alexander. Forgive me, Lord, but I hated her. Very softly, she added, "Herez, where you, Herez?"

She turned back toward her chair and Bosco stepped forward: "Now we want to hear a few words from the mother of Baltharzar King, whose body has never been found."

Bosco went to the left of the microphone where Mistee Unrickety sat. With showy courtliness, he put his hand under her elbow and helped her up. She too leaned heavily on him. Placing her in front of the microphone, which he solicitously lowered for her, he stepped back and clasped his hands in front of him.

"Friends of little Baltharzar," she almost whispered into the mike. "My friends."

The effect was electric. The crowd made a rushing ahsound like each person felt at once the power of the moment and had to breathe in to have enough air to go on.

Then they fell silent, their faces open, expectant.

"Some of you knew my baby. The papers and the TV talk about him not having legs. He had a big heart, though, and he love me and I love him. You love somethin' that can't take care for itself special, and Baltharzar couldn't walk." She paused. "When I think . . ." she paused again; "When I think of what mean people could do to a poor cripple boy . . . ." Her voice faltered and she looked at Bosco. He went forward and stood respectfully behind her in case he's got to catch her falling body. Then she resumed, "When Baltharzar disappeared, I had to go away a little while. I was so upset I had to go see my sister so's I wouldn't go crazy. But I'm back now and I want justice for Baltharzar, for my sweet crippled baby. My maw used to say Baltharzar the sweetest child ever draw breath. That's the God's truth. My Baltharzar the sweetest thing and he taken from me. Taken from me. Who knows what done been done to him now? Maybe he got French fries stuck up in him and he layin' in the land fill. Maybe his little stumps of legs be in rottin' Burger Bin sacks, the kind what say 'Have a Good Day, the Burger Bin Way.' We want this city to do right by my baby, by all our chi'ren, and we want it now. Like Bosco say, 'We want to find our chi'ren. Now. We got to dig for our chi'ren. Now.'"

She slid back to collapse into Bosco's arms while the crowd began to swell with the chant: "Find our children. Dig for our children. Now. Dig for our children. Now. Dig, now. Dig, now. Dig. Dig. Dig. Now."

Mistee was quite a performer and somebody had told her the right moves. Someone had written her a good script, too, especially the have-a-good-day sacks from the Burger Bin.

People at other apartments where Mistee lived had noticed that Baltharzar was missing. He was certainly easy to spot. They reported him missing. But since there was no trace of his mother or stepfather either, the police had been slow to add Baltharzar's name to the list of missing persons. It looked like the whole family had moved. But then when plans for the Mothers' Rally spread, Mistee Unrickety appeared. She had pictures of Baltharzar, and my office staff—of all people—easily corroborated from our records that Mistee Unrickety was Baltharzar King's mother.

"Find our children. Find our boys. Dig for our boys. Dig. Now." The lines filled the screen as reporters and commentators offered their views of the demonstration and on Manchester's Mothers for Justice.

The bossman for this place interrupted me. All I can say to him is, "Thank you, no. I've made my peace with the Lord. Yes, I'm still writing. Just some personal papers to pass the time." He has that suspicious look. A middle-aged woman writing with a little ol' plastic ink pen can't be somethin' terrible.

The papers and the TV made sure there was a public record. All kinds of people covered the trial. And wrote up what happened in languages I couldn't begin to read. The public record, I learned in social services, never tells much. It has its own truth, kind of a truth that lies because it misses the motives and the faces and the horrible feeling folks get way down in their stomachs. Records miss reasons just like forms miss the very thing they are supposed to pinpoint. Getting the personal truth is the hard part.

What happened in the kitchen that morning just before I stopped being a public servant and became public property matters, seems to me. That's the inside story of a real quiet, peaceful day.

At the kitchen table on a Saturday morning I poured another cup of coffee and folded back the *Manchester Daily Banner*. Every column on every page of the whole section eye-balled the trial of Travis Mozell or worked at figuring him out. Folks had to get at his motives. They wanted to get inside his head. And though I knew he was wrong, I hated that he didn't have any privacy left. He didn't belong to himself. A couple of reporters kept focusing on pattern and what the pattern in serial killers said about Travis.

They talked about a serial killer in one part of the country and a killer in another, a killer up East, and a killer in the Rockies. Made it seem serial killers were like big shopping malls, all alike no matter where you went. Made it sound like all minds are alike. Like you went in and purchased your motive at a mall and had it dropped in a plastic bag with a cutout place for a handle. I didn't take to the term *serial killer*, and I sure didn't cotton that all minds and motives pretty well matched, but I kept reading.

Most of the headlines looked familiar. The press recalled traces of hair, fiber, even curly excelsior from big packing crates and the way serial killers couldn't shed those things. Traces, they said—like some whisper you could touch on Travis's clothing and in his room, stuff he carried around with him and marked with. Lord, for a minute or two I thought I might be reading about tom cats with all that marking of spots. Serial killers, according to the experts, left a trail of traces. Kind of like children in fairy tales dropping crumbs, I fancied. Of course the crumbs were supposed to help them find their way back, and the killers were losing their way. They were going towards the witch's house or the monster's cave, not back home where smoke curled up out the chimney and lettuce and beans grew in the garden. Here was a trail: the condiments and Burger Bin napkins on Charlton Luther's body, the foil wrappers, bags, and little packets from the Burger Bin on Jingle Sprinkle's.

Then all kinds of other things caused trouble. At least eight inches in the paper claimed that the case would have to be moved because one lawyer failed to call Travis *Mr. Mozell*. All these words about one word. All this to-do that failure to use *Mr.* showed such prejudice Travis couldn't begin to get a fair hearing. *Mr.,* indeed, I mused over my coffee.

One headline was what I'd been expecting: "Profile of Victims: Sad Pasts, Low Horizons." I didn't expect to learn anything I didn't know about children of desolate pasts and desperate futures, but I wanted to hear it from a newspaper, not a social work text or my own files.

I read "Profile" word by word:

The addition of Charlton Luther and Jingle Sprinkle, the first bodies found after the Burger Bin Massacre of September 1987, has added to the weight of evidence against Travis Mozell, held as the gunman who killed eight people at the Burger Bin on Old Dixie Avenue. The similarity between these boys and those who disappeared several years ago has prompted the police and the FBI, called in at the request of the governor, to review all the evidence assembled when Herez Alexander, Baltharzar King, and Enamel Toney were reported missing. The five boys had much in common, but evidence is too scanty to pursue conviction. All the youths reported missing or known murdered suffered from serious handicaps and had little chance for futures that could be fulfilling. All had such limited abilities that no career or even steady work would be open to them. Years of poverty, welfare, and confusion seemed virtually certain. Institutionalization would have been probable for those that social service agencies pursued.

Suggested as victims of Travis Mozell, all of these youths were primarily victims of society and parental abuse. Like any other children they were innocent and could not define or fight for their rights; unlike others they had few defenders because they were outside the arm of regular school systems. Retardation, either from genetic flaw or environmental influence, set them apart, and their isolation led directly to their being preyed upon by perpetrators of street crime and murder.

At least they are beyond those dangers now.

After I read that piece—terribly unfair because it practically said Mozell killed my sons—I put the paper down and refilled my coffee cup. Picking the section back up, I found a page of letters to the editor. Some were indignant, some ridiculous, the way such letters usually run; but one got to me. A woman in Eastmont wrote that she'd followed all the accounts in the paper and didn't believe Travis Mozell was guilty of the deaths of any of the missing boys because from the Burger Bin Massacre and the state of Luther's and Sprinkle's bodies, Mozell seemed extroverted and violent, someone interested in sensation and spectacle. She maintained that whoever concentrated on boys like the three missing ones had to be an angel in disguise, someone who wanted to spare them additional suffering. "Those children," she wrote, "are not only free from the abuse of their people and community and of the institutions in which they would eventually be incarcerated but they are also symbols—flaming swords to lead us to improve child care and eradicate poverty." Then she went off into some fanatical program that no social services budget in the world could ever sustain.

I came to the next article in the *Daily Banner*.

FBI investigators on special assignment reported that the case of Meroney Espy, whose body was found between the discovery of those of Luther and Sprinkle, had been solved. His father and stepmother had killed him because he was a "nuisance," according to the FBI.

Billy Espy and his common-law wife, Raynelle Cox, tried to cover their guilt by linking the disappearance of the child with the slayings. The so-called nuisance required a great deal of attention because of his handicap.

Meroney Espy, a hydrocephalic, was kept bound to a chair for eight hours at a time because he repeatedly banged his head against the wall. He could neither feed nor clean himself, yet his father refused to release him into protective custody. Billy Espy wanted the support money paid him for Meroney. Apparently the elder Espy thought he could dispose of the boy, keep the death a secret, and continue to collect the money.

City social service employees became suspicious when they served papers to have Meroney removed from the house for his own safety and could not find the child. Billy Espy then claimed Meroney had been kidnapped.

Meroney Espy is not atypical of the boys, aged 5 to 11, who disappeared between 1979 and 1984, and for whom no evidence has been found, and the two recently recovered bodies in or near the dumpsters of Burger Bin, one on the extreme south side of Manchester, one thirty miles away near the fast-food eatery in Olympia.

At the top of the editorial page, of the same issue of the *Daily Banner*, I saw the headline: "Herez Alexander's Disappearance Still a Mystery."

Herez Alexander disappeared in March 1979, and his body has never been found. His case is conspicuous because his mother, Molly Alexander, failed to report him missing until the case attracted national attention, at which time Ms. Alexander claimed her son had been kidnapped and killed.

Ms. Alexander, of D-38 Calvin Court, was able, however, to fix the date on which she had last seen the boy—March 1979. She explained that she did not report him missing because she assumed Herez's father, whom she had not seen in five years, had taken the boy for a visit with him.

Herez was eleven years old, but according to the records at Children's Services, which had tried to help the family, the boy had a mental age of five. Tests suggested that he might be taught to take care of himself but little more. Physically stunted as well, he could not do manual labor.

A young caseworker at the center remembers Herez as a boy who responded to attention the way a small animal might, but with no cognitive comprehension of his environment. The caseworker, who asked not to be identified, went on to say that life held little promise for Herez and that if he was dead, she hoped it was painless. "I feel about him like I do about many old people. I just don't want them to suffer. Death is a blessing."

That's strong language for a specialist in social work.

I read the other editorials, then the rest of the letters

and articles, and then sat at the kitchen table and looked out at my yard. It really was more beautiful than I remembered it in earlier springs. The gold-spotted aucuba made a tall thick screen that gave us privacy and Lon and his family privacy. I couldn't see his truck or old cars. Behind the aucuba and in the corner of the lot the azaleas made a triangle of green and white. In front of the big bushes Gus had salvaged were the small plants I'd added. The white blooms in the dark green foliage made the area strong and clean. I was glad I'd used only white plants. They were banked like an altar, simple but stately.

Two birds strutted on the white bench in front of the azaleas. I glanced up to make sure the bird feeder had plenty of seeds. Plenty. And the new feeders kept the squirrels from taking what was not meant for them and then scattering the remaining seeds so the birds couldn't get them.

The sundial Janeece loved to talk with stood not far from the white bench. From my window I couldn't see the angle of the shadow or the old Roman numerals on its face, but I watched a mockingbird land and balance for just a moment on the tip of the hour shaft. The soft gray of the bird blended with the sundial, and I knew the tiny bird body changed the shadow cast. I knew we had to move with the light.

How much the Nellie Stevens hollies had grown surprised me. Across the back of the fence they were a dark and lustrous, impenetrable hedge. While I could sometimes hear the people who lived behind me, I couldn't see them, so secure and protective was my sanctuary. In the

flush of spring the right corner was best. The Bradford
pear spread out its umbrella of lace and leaf sure that
sunshine and shower would go on forever for it and the
hundreds of tulips underneath.

To the right, masking the gate and the garbage cans,
were more azaleas and daylilies. From the kitchen I couldn't
see it, of course, but I knew the Grancy grey-beard was
blooming out front, surrounded by velvety purple pansies.

Below the garden, the boys lay—Herez, Baltharzar,
Enamel. Plants in tribute to him made a home for Peter as
well. The boys were as much a part of spring as the
Bradford pear and the Grancy grey-beard. Their winter of
abuse was over and the days or years that might have been
theirs would work neither killing rot nor frost.

I'd killed four little boys. Three lay in the spring
garden and Peter swung high in a distant magnolia grove.
I'd broken not just the civic law described in article after
article this morning but also ancient and divine codes. But
I felt neither guilt nor remorse; rather, I knew with a calm,
deep confidence that I'd done the best possible thing for
those little boys, so severely handicapped, so seriously
abused and neglected.

I sat there hours thinking about the little boys and
drawing peace from my garden. I thought about my years
in children's services and the sense of rightness in what I'd
done. I'd honored all my professional obligations because
I'd matched conditions and opportunities.

All those years—the food I'd donated, the money I'd
given, the programs in which I'd enrolled young people,
the trips I'd made, the funds I'd solicited from business

and industry, the letters of recommendation, the clothes, the children I'd kept, the grants for child-care I applied for and got, the fees I'd paid to send children to camp or to take music or dancing lessons. I had a good record for doing what would benefit a child most. My office wall was covered with certificates that said so.

I kept the pattern, giving Herez and the others what could help them most, in fact, the only thing that could help them—freedom from their multiple cages. Freedom, not graves, was in the garden.

I remember my father preaching about gardens. Sometimes he'd get lost in his own sentences as he tried to convey the great glory and goodness of Eden and how much we'd lost by sinning. I wished he could see my garden. It conveyed to me what all his sermons and all his lessons hadn't; but then I know his teaching prepared the soil for my garden.

Was the little yard with its azaleas and tulips, its Bradford pear and its talking sundial a place of a fall for me, the way Daddy said the first garden was? No. I don't believe so. Not in the ways he meant. But the terms I would apply to my garden are not ones my father would consider: Rightness. Freedom. Vindication. Air. The pear tree swaying its limbs whispered I'd done right in freeing. The leaves whispered "freedom" and vindicated me and my acts.

At no point did I doubt that I'd done the right thing for the boys, though I realized that the law would have to rule otherwise.

The special section of the *Daily Banner*, with its

coverage of Travis Mozell, lay open on the table next to the pig-shaped salt and pepper shakers. The picture of my Josie was there. And truth was in the garden. My life was fine. I loved my work. I was making a difference in people's lives. I had what I needed. I had adopted two adorable little girls, whom I loved more than I ever believed I could love. I had lost one to Travis Mozell, who, cocaine-crazed, gunned her down. She was innocent and harmless, a child who had suffered. The other, off today at her one-Saturday-a-month art camp, gave every sign of having an extremely high IQ, a remarkable talent in art, and a spirit that would in time free itself from the dark shadows and terrible scars of her first five years. I needed to help her grow up. I had obligations to the future already. Janeece shouldn't have to be wounded any more. She shouldn't be the object of scorn and interviews and prying because of what I'd done. She shouldn't have to know that the garden she loved so much was the burial site of three boys—by extension her beloved siblings. I had obligations to Janeece. I had everything, all the worthwhile things most people measure by; furthermore, I had truth in the garden. I could look forward to years of meaningful work, a good retirement, years of watching Janeece flourish and achieve. My health was excellent, my mind clear, and my heart brimming.

But truth was not just in the garden. Truth was what Travis Mozell needed. All those foil wrappers and packages of salt and catsup apply only to Charlton Luther and Jingle Sprinkle, not to the missing children, most definitely not to Herez Alexander, who has more attention given him in this one newspaper than was ever his in the eleven years of his life, or to Baltharzar King, or to Enamel Toney.

Mothers like Molly Alexander and Mistee Unrickety came into national prominence and transmuted their neglect and abuse into injured and deprived maternity. They denied their children a minimum of attention and now greedily sought the sympathy of the nation. I didn't understand it, but I understood what I had to do.

The light had shifted. I had to move with the light.

Travis Mozell was one of my boys too.

Boy. I called him *boy*, it didn't make him less or me unjust. I didn't have to call him *Mr.*

Travis, boy, son—any of them good words. *Son* was fine. *Boy* was fine. Either one suggested age and duty and affection. Maybe they were all my sons. And I had to do what would be best for him. I had to choose what would help him, and what he needed was not to be blamed for or even suspected of murders that he didn't commit. The tokens from the fast-food chain were not definitive evidence; the authorities admitted that his case was only somewhat like those of serial killers who matched shopping malls. There was a good chance of focusing just on the shooting in the restaurant, not on the bodies found in the dumpsters. Still, I knew as his trial progressed, someone, using the sociological and psychological profiles of Luther and Sprinkle as evidence, would at least insinuate there in court, not just in a rally or a letter to the editor, that Travis Mozell had killed the missing boys, too. I know how the system works.

I could see to it that three cases would never help send Travis Mozell to the chair—even though he was going to the chair anyway, in all probability. Guilt in the fast-food killings seemed indisputable. Guilt for killing my Josie. I could identify him; I saw him clearly that day in the Burger Bin. My God! I could identify him. When I looked at the photo of just his face that first time, I hadn't been sure, but now I was. I'd seen him move on TV and in court, and the movement was the same. The fact hit me for the first time. I could send him to the chair because my word and my position would carry weight. I could send him to the chair, and I was worried about the three boys in the garden. With Travis Mozell gone, no one would ever wonder about Herez, Baltharzar, and Enamel.

There was no need to involve Peter. No notification of his being missing had ever surfaced, and the couple from the Kmart had disappeared. But the three in the garden had an identity because two of the mothers believed that money and fame could grow from the tears of their weeping. I knew them; I knew their style.

But I had a motive and that was to see that justice went as far as I could help justice go. The light had shifted and I had to keep my three boys off Travis Mozell's docket. Lord, it was a strange debate. I had to keep the record of the murderer of my little girl as clear as possible so he wouldn't be convicted unjustly. To do the right thing by him, I had to uproot my life and do harm to Janeece. And I would have as hard a time proving my guilt as Mozell would his innocence because my record was as sterling in service as his was questionable. Doing Right

Hold Steady. The old line, the one my folks always teased me about, still operated. I had to call the law and do as right by justice as I had by love. A garden is a fine place to realize such truths.

I opened my Old Testament and read Isaiah 61:11, "For as the earth bringeth forth her bud, and as the garden causeth the things that are sown in it to spring forth; so the Lord God will cause righteousness and praise to spring forth before all the nations."

First I called my niece Martha in Augusta and told her she wouldn't want to believe what would happen in the next few days, but I needed her to come right now and get Jan and keep her safe. She knew all my legal and financial affairs. I'd provided as well as I could for both Jan and Martha as her guardian.

Then I called the Manchester Police Department. It took all day because everyone thought I was a prankster.

Once the news broke, the newspapers carried little else. My picture was everywhere. Everything I have ever done was the subject of scrutiny, speculation, interpretation. I lost myself. I became public property. But what hurt most was the garden. They dug it up. They wrecked it so that leaf and branch were at odds, and the order and peace I'd achieved fell into a mass of red clay mounds. The roots of the big bushes were left in the air to wither. I knew I'd never see it again, never face the task of setting it to rights again, but when they took me to verify that they'd dug in all the right spots, I grieved the rape of the earth. The system had done to the garden what it would have done to the innocent boys—distorted and destroyed them.

So the boys got it finally—in form if not in feeling. The feeling, at least, I spared them.

I saw the wreck of the garden and thought of my old father. The sundial lay broken, its circular and numbered top upside down so that light would never again strike its shaft. All that remained for me was the final day in court.

The judge and I went a long way back together. He was a black judge, one of the first. We'd been on civic boards together. We'd tried, in community service, to help others. We'd kept a kind of simple faith from our humble origins that hard work and high standards would make a difference.

He looked like an ancient prophet, his dark face and grizzled hair above the black robe; but I was close enough to see his eyes. They were filled with tears.

Controlling his voice, Judge Blevins asked, "Ms. Putman, how do you plead?"

The court was absolutely still.

I looked at him and said as if it were the "I do" of a marriage ceremony: "Guilty, Your Honor."

He swallowed and paused in the swamping silence. Then: "By reason of insanity?"

He wants me to have an out, I registered. The air hung heavy between us. "No, Your Honor. By reason of charity." He met my eyes for just a moment and then looked down. I could hear the press corps rushing from the court. I knew how the headlines would read: "Guilty By Reason of Charity."

Day Six

The pulp magazines like to talk about irony. They see some big difference between me as a woman that received recognition for my services to children and me as a mad woman who disposed of children in the garden. Crazy folks like to accuse me of being mentally ill, of suffering from a split personality. I read something called "The Many Faces of Genia Putman" just the other day.

In the trial, some psychiatrist said he could use my speech to prove I suffered from multiple personalities. Lord, how dim he was. He had ears but could not hear. He stayed on the witness stand a long time and pretended to make a case that I was mentally unfit to stand trial. What he was really doing was showing off. You work with as many smart-aleck children as I have and you spot the showing off real quick.

He tried to make the jury believe that I had three voices, one each for my personalities. He said something like "At times the defendant speaks in standard English and uses, carefully and correctly, the professional vocabulary of social services. We have a record of these voices from the speeches she made to government officials, in taking awards, and in offering plans and procedures. But on other occasions, she assumes rural black speech and practices the dropped endings, the incorrect verb forms, and accents on the first syllable. All of these show the assertion of another personality."

He pronounced some words in what he thought of as cornfield speech: *knowed*, *po*-lice, *Hit don't*. He made some sentences with *be* as the verb. And he looked mighty smug when he did it, like he was some high-powered linguist that knew what he was talking about. Lord, Lord, he ought to know that a verb don't have to have the right ending to cut right through to what matters about life and that most folks, in the grieving time, drop their school words like a snake shedding a useless skin, because those words might get you a job but they don't tote a load of meaning.

What was funniest was his idea of my third voice. I remember exactly what he said because it shocked me so and took me back to the time I was fifteen or so and thought I could be some great black woman poet. That fool psychiatrist stood up in court—and, Lord forgive me, I know he was trying to get me off as mentally unfit—but he'd get up in court and, say: "The defendant assumes another personality and speaks in another voice. The black speech falls into a kind of chant, a soul-call of forceful repetition. She speaks in images of gardens or rising and falling, of giving and getting with which the Bible is stitched together. The Hebraic call, the King James rhythms, and the old black preacher's roll call are not the voice of a stable woman of the end of the twentieth century. She speaks in tongues."

That's what he said. Lord, Lord. All he had to do was ask me and I could of told him about my growing up, my daddy preaching, my folks telling me to do well in school, the school telling me to talk white in the white world if I wanted to get ahead. Three voices. He be right about that, but three personalities? No. All three are my voice. They weave together like a braid, a thick black braid size of a good rope.

That jury knew I had one mind, but I have a feeling they thought the psychiatrist had turned funny.

Even now when respected newspapers look back at the case, the writers stress how vulnerable the children were and how vulnerable the children of certain groups and geographical pockets remain. The writers always say the children belong to a group that seemed waiting for a tragedy to happen. In the hopelessness of most housing projects, the papers stress, only the best and the brightest have the strength and the resourcefulness to hustle odd jobs or collect cans at shopping areas and filling stations. All I did was cross paths with a few who couldn't hustle or collect cans. I dipped into the world I knew best and came up with those beyond the usual categories of the welfare system, but not beyond the heart. It's not so hard now that I look back. I was doing my job, and suddenly, right there, in my house, in my own kitchen, was a little boy I could help in a way that all the forms, committees, and grants couldn't. And I know how it sounds. Makes me sound crazy. I know that.

It can't be long before some guard will come to my cell and tell me it's time. I've even read accounts in the paper on how rare it is for a woman to go to the chair. Apparently, a good many rare things defined my life.

What else could I do with the last six days of my life except keep a journal that put down how much I loved my children? Doors open and close, and the very swinging of them—opening and closing in time—gave me a little time to fulfill the dream of writing, and come to think of it, of making a special garden. Didn't make the garden the way I wanted to as a tomboy girl who hankered to be a horticulturist, when she didn't have a glimmer of what that meant or a ghost of doing it. And this journal I've kept in six days is not what I thought I meant by writing when I saw myself as Langston Hughes or James Weldon Johnson. But at fifty I have a good bit more to reflect on than I did at fifteen. If, then, I looked forward to writing, I now look back to write.

By tomorrow these sheets probably be in the trash. Or maybe Martha and Jan get my "personal effects." Don't know what they'd do with them, but Jan, some day, might like to know my mind. Or she may need to forget. She may never have to decide. I don't know the official policy of disposing of the worldly goods and personal papers of women sent to the chair for love.

ABOUT THE AUTHOR

JoAllen Bradham, who received her Ph.D. from Vanderbilt University, is a member of the creative writing faculty at Kennesaw State University in Atlanta. She won the 1994 Breakthrough Award in Southern and Southwestern Fiction, and the Texas Review Press edition of *Some Personal Papers* won the 1996 Townsend Award. Bradham has published short stories, poems, and essays, and her plays have won several competitions, including the Tennessee Williams Ten-Minute Play Competition.